GLOBAL WARNING

STEVEN B. FRANK

CLARION BOOKS
An Imprint of HarperCollinsPublishers

For climate warriors everywhere—especially the
young ones leading the way

Clarion Books is an imprint of HarperCollins Publishers.

Global Warning
Copyright © 2023 by Steven B. Frank
Quotation on page 44 by David Attenborough from
David Attenborough: A Life on Our Planet, 2020.
For information address HarperCollins Children's Books, a division of HarperCollins Publishers, 195 Broadway, New York, NY 10007.
www.harpercollinschildrens.com

Library of Congress Cataloging-in-Publication Data
Names: Frank, Steven, 1963– author.
Title: Global warning / Steven B. Frank.
Description: First edition. | New York : Clarion Books, 2023. | Audience: Ages
   8–12. | Audience: Grades 4–6. | Summary: Five seventh-graders concerned
   about climate change work with a retired lawyer and an activist grandmother
   to build an international movement to amend the United States Constitution,
   protecting humanity's right to live on a planet free of pollution and warming.
Identifiers: LCCN 2022036198 | ISBN 9780358566175 (hardcover)
Subjects: CYAC: Environmentalism—Fiction. | Student movements—Fiction. |
   Environmental law—Fiction.
Classification: LCC PZ7.1.F746 Gl 2023 | DDC [Fic]—dc23
LC record available at https://lccn.loc.gov/2022036198

Typography by David Hastings
23 24 25 26 27 LBC 5 4 3 2 1

First Edition

Young people—they care.

—DAVID ATTENBOROUGH

1

I Have to Download the Anxiety App Again

"Sam, smell my hair."

Catalina leans in close. She probably tried a new shampoo last night and wants to know how it smells to the world. What better way than to ask a friend who would never lie to her?

But I'm about to lie to her. Because her hair smells like lighter fluid.

"Smells nice, Cat. New shampoo?"

She gives me a look.

"Reminds me of summer. The Fourth of July. Burgers on the grill."

"That's the stink of jet fuel. Fifteen thousand gallons dumped from the sky onto the playground at my sister's school. I spent a whole hour with her in the bath, washing her hair. She was so freaked-out, she slept in my bed."

We hear the roar of a jet engine overhead, and we look up.

Catalina's little sister's school isn't the only one in a flight path. Our middle school is just a few miles from the Hollywood Burbank Airport.

"Why would a jet dump fuel on a schoolyard?"

"Engine trouble, they said. They had to turn around but were too heavy to land. So they dumped fuel."

"On kids?"

"And their teachers. And a whole neighborhood. *My* neighborhood. The school is going to sue the airline."

Anytime I hear the word *sue,* part of me wakes up. It reminds me of what we did last year to stop homework. My friends Alistair, Jaesang, Catalina, and me, along with my big sister, Sadie, and her boyfriend, Sean, filed a class action lawsuit against the school board. We argued that kids have a constitutional right to a childhood and that homework was taking away that right. With a *lot* of legal help from our neighbor, Mr. Kalman, we took our case all the way to the Supreme Court. That made me very anxious. But it was worth it.

Alistair comes over to our regular lunch table. It's under Jaesang's favorite tree, a magnolia. We like its shade all through the school year and its white blossoms when summer is just a month away.

Instead of saying hi or good morning, Alistair greets us

with, "Know how many animals died in the Australian wildfires? A billion. We're not talking about common roadkill, either. These animals are *cute*. Koalas. Kangaroos. Wallabies. *Wallabies!* I used to sleep with a stuffy of one. Named her Julia."

For Julia Child, one of Alistair's top-five favorite chefs.

"Used to?" I say.

"Well . . . my seventh-grade resolution is to leave her on the shelf."

Then he makes us watch a YouTube about the fires.

Alistair's always doing that, shoving a video in my face before I have a chance to say yes, that's something I want in my head, or no thanks, I'd rather not. I appreciate how enthusiastic he gets for the right cause, but some things activate my anxiety.

Like baby koalas with burnt paws.

I can't look away. Neither, it seems, can Alistair. He stands beside me, watching. He starts to cry.

"Alistair," I say.

"I can't help it, Sam. I've seen it twenty times. Each time, it shatters me."

He puts his head on my shoulder and weeps.

"Please, don't."

"What's wrong with crying? Crying is caring."

"You're getting my shirt wet."

He lifts his head from the wet spot on my Miles Davis T-shirt just as Jaesang walks up.

"What's he crying about?" Jaesang says.

"Burnt koalas," Catalina says.

"Want to cry some more? Look at this." Jaesang holds up his phone to show a satellite image of a hurricane forming in the Atlantic. It's this massive swirl of clouds headed for the Eastern Seaboard.

"That's Clyde. The third named tropical storm of the season. Meteorologists think he'll be a Category Four by the time he makes landfall in Florida."

Jaesang used to want to own the Lakers someday. But when Kobe fell from the sky, he got so depressed he dropped his dream of owning an NBA team. Now his passion is the weather. His grandfather bought him a Falcon weather station with wind speed monitor, barometer, soil monitor, rain gauge, and hygrometer. All the basketball stats in his brain turned into facts about the weather.

I wonder if he ever thinks about the bad weather that brought down Kobe's helicopter.

"Did you know that when the World Meteorological Organization names tropical storms, it can reuse names after six years, but it never reuses the names of the truly awesome ones?"

"Why not?"

"Out of respect for the people who died or lost their homes."

"Kind of like the NBA retiring the jerseys of the really great players," Alistair says. I love Alistair, but sometimes food isn't the only thing that lands in his mouth. This time it's his foot.

But the thing about Jaesang . . . he's strong inside and out. "Yeah," he says. "There'll never be another Katrina. Or Kobe."

Jae also tracks temperatures. "Last summer it hit 114 degrees in Portland, Oregon, 80 in the Arctic, 120 in Sicily, 130 in Death Valley. And for a week in winter, Dallas was colder than Anchorage. The planet is discombobulated. Even Mount Shasta lost all its snow. The UN climate report calls it *code red for humanity*. And it's all our fault."

It gets quiet at our table. We look around the schoolyard. Trash cans filled past the top. Kids playing handball, cramming for quizzes, hanging out. It's code red for humanity, but life seems to just go on.

"You know we could reduce greenhouse gases by twenty percent if we all stopped eating meat?" Alistair says.

"Are *you* going to stop eating meat, MasterChef Junior?" Catalina asks. That's been Cat's nickname for Alistair since he actually went on the show—and won.

"Already have. I got inspired by Greta."

He pulls *Time* magazine's Person of the Year issue out of his backpack, touches the front cover, a picture of the climate change activist Greta Thunberg, then touches his fingers to his lips.

"Ask me anything about her."

"What's the name of her—"

"Dogs? Roxy and Moses. Boat? *La Vagabonde*. Sister? Beata."

"When did she first get depressed over cli—"

"Third grade. Her teacher showed her a video. It wrecked her."

"What kind of work does her mom—"

"Opera singer. Greta flygskammed her—that's Swedish for flight shamed—and now she takes the train to all her performances."

"How tall—"

"Five feet. But she stands tall to power. One day she sat herself down in front of the Swedish parliament with a sign: SCHOOL STRIKE FOR THE PLANET. One person one day. Two people the next. Then twenty more. Then a few hundred. Then, all over the world, millions knew about her. Have you guys heard her TED talks? They kill me every time. And she makes this little sound when she pauses. Not everyone can hear it, but I can. A soft grunt, like she's getting control of her anger. A tiny exhale of total poise. That sound . . . That girl . . . Man, what I wouldn't give to cook for her. Just one meal."

"Alistair," Catalina says, "I think you're in love."

• • •

After school, I'm on my bike, riding home, when I see a for sale sign in front of Mr. Kalman's house. Naturally I assume the worst. I always do. He probably fell, hit his head, and died. He promised my mom that when he was gone, she could have the listing. Sure enough, there's Jenny Warren's face on the sign. And there goes my career as Mr. Kalman's handyman, water boy, and tech guy—a trifecta of odd jobs that have made me reasonably rich for a twelve-year-old.

But how can I be thinking of lost income at a time like this? I've lost a friend, our legal leader who was like a grandpa to us.

Or is this one of Mr. Kalman's stunts? He always likes to keep us guessing.

I hop off my bike in front of his house. His *Los Angeles Times* is still on the driveway. I used to pick it up out of the gutter sludge and walk it to his front door. Seeing it now, on his driveway, I think, This isn't a stunt. He's really gone.

I start to cry.

I Facetime Sadie. She's in her first year of college at Brown. She answers in a library and has to whisper.

"Sam, what's the matter?"

"This."

I flip the camera around to show her the newspaper on the driveway, our mom's face on the for sale sign.

"I know," she says. "Mom told me."

"Why'd she tell you and not me?"

"I think they were waiting to tell you in person. I'm sorry, Sam. I know how much you'll miss him."

"When did this even happen?"

"Well, you know he promised Mom the listing."

"I don't mean that. I mean, when did Mr. Kalman die?"

The screen freezes. *Poor connection.*

I try to reconnect. Must be in a dead zone. That's appropriate.

So I cry alone.

"Did the mail come?"

I look up and see a ghost in track pants, a Brown University sweatshirt, and a scarf. When he was alive, he always complained about the cold.

"Mr. Kalman? What . . . I mean, I thought—"

"You thought your mom would have sold the house in one day? She's a good realtor, Sam, but not that good."

8
★

"No. I thought you were dead."

"Just downsizing. An apartment became available at a senior housing complex nearby. Not, mind you, an assisted-living facility like your sister tried to push me into. This is an apartment building for independent seniors. The NoHo Senior Arts Colony. There's a theater, a pool, weekly movie night, yoga classes, a ceramics studio, and a writers' group for those with a story to tell. I may take up yoga."

He peeks inside his mailbox, empty, and looks up at me.

"I'm afraid, Sam, that I won't be needing your gardening services anymore. I apologize for the loss of income. You're welcome to use me as a reference."

"That's okay, Mr. Kalman. At least you're still alive."

He starts to head back into his house, then stops and says, "I could use a little help unpacking tomorrow. The NoHo Senior Arts Colony. Apartment 303. Come by around ten."

• • •

That night, I have a hard time falling asleep. I keep thinking of little kids whose hair stinks of jet fuel. Deadly storms brewing in the Atlantic. And that koala with charred fur. More of Alistair's videos pop into my head: a polar bear frantically paddling in search of ice, levees in New Orleans breached by seawater, dead puffins washed up on an Arctic shore, and forests full of dry, brown trees.

And then I see the face of Alistair's crush, the Person of the Year who's fighting for the planet's survival. I start to worry. What if she fails? What if our future is a Noah's Ark–size flood, only there won't even be two of each animal left to save?

I reach for my phone, tap the App Store, and download the anxiety app again. The guided meditation lady tells me to breathe, and I wonder, what kind of air?

2

Somebody Gets Arrested

Mr. Kalman wasn't kidding. At the NoHo Senior Arts Colony, they have yoga, movie night, and memoir writing. The bulletin board in the elevator makes this place look fun.

I press 3 for his floor. The doors start to close, but a voice calls out—

"Can you hold that?"

I stick my hand between the closing doors. They open again.

A girl with purple highlights in her short hair comes riding up on a skateboard. She turns back, calls out, "Nana, elevator's here," and kicks up her board.

"Betty's slow, but she never falls," she says. Sure enough, around the corner comes an older lady pushing a walker. Not one of those depressing gray metal walkers with tennis balls on the feet. This looks like something a kid would dream up, a cross between a skateboard and a bike, with a seat in case the old person gets tired—or wants to transport a bag of fertilizer and a tin watering can.

They must've walked all the way from the nursery.

"Thank you for holding it," the woman says. "Not everyone does." She glances at the panel. "We're on four."

The elevator is slow to lift off. Probably it's programmed that way so the seniors don't pass out from a sudden jump in altitude. The slow ascent gives me a chance to notice that the grandma is pretty chic in khaki pants, white sweater, orange scarf, and blue suede Adidas. She's wearing a baseball cap, too, that says RATIFY THE ERA.

I'm not sure what it means to ratify an era, but I'll ask Mr. Kalman.

"We forgot the cages for the tomatoes," the grandma says.

"We won't need them for"—Skateboard Girl glances at a seed packet in her hand—"seventy-five days. At least."

"If I get a craving for tomatoes, there's always Instacart."

"They'll taste better from your own balcony, Nana. Promise."

The car stops, the doors open, and I step out. I head down the hall, around the corner, to apartment 303. I ring the doorbell, and soon the door opens.

Mr. Kalman waves hello with a hammer.

"Need help hanging pictures?" I say.

In his house, he had a wall full of photographs of all his clients, mostly kids whose cases he argued in court. There was one of me and Alistair and Jaesang and Catalina and Sadie and Sean on the steps of the U.S. Supreme Court. The day we organized a Million Kid March.

"Something like that."

He leans out, looks up the hall and down, sees that we're alone.

"It's a mezuzah."

"Wait, a what?"

"Mezuzah. A tiny Torah scroll encased in glass or metal. It gets hung on the doorpost of a Jewish home."

He holds out a small glass that has a rolled-up paper inside and a couple of thin nails.

"I get it. You can't see the nail."

"It's true that my eyesight isn't good enough to hammer a small nail," Mr. Kalman says, "but it *is* good enough to read the fine print on my lease, which prohibits hammering outside the apartment. Problem is, according to Jewish law, the mezuzah has to hang outside the door."

"The lease is unconstitutional, then," I say. "It infringes on your religious freedom."

Mr. Kalman smiles. He's taught me well.

"But do we really want to drag the management to court for a thing like this?"

"*De minimus non curat lex,*" I say. "The law does not concern itself with trifles."

"Exactly. So it'll be better if *you* hang the mezuzah. That way, if anyone gets in trouble, it won't be me."

There's another Latin legal term he taught us, *qui facit per alium facit per se.* He who acts through another, acts for himself. But I decide to keep that one to myself.

"Where do you want it?" I ask, taking the hammer.

"Halfway from your head to the ceiling."

I put the mezuzah against the doorframe and slide it up.

"A little lower. You've grown."

I bring it down a few inches.

"Good. Now slide the bottom edge forty-five degrees to the right. It's supposed to be on a slant. That's it. Hold it right there. But don't swing. Wait for the music."

He heads back into the apartment and turns on his record player. I don't know what the fine print in his lease says about loud music on a Saturday morning, but I doubt he's in compliance. Suddenly Count Basie brass is blasting into the room.

Mr. Kalman gives me the thumbs-up, and I swing. The nails go in easy—two taps each—and we're in the clear.

He lowers the music, and I look around the apartment. "Where are all the boxes?"

"In the Buick."

The Buick is Mr. Kalman's classic station wagon from the 1970s. *A cream puff of a car. A handy hauler. A real workhorse.* Those are some of his nicknames for the Buick. We love it for its tape deck and his collection of cassettes. And for the stories it reminds him to tell.

"Where's the Buick?"

"Donated."

"What?"

"To KCRW. They took care of all the paperwork. She was too thirsty for gas, Sam. And anyway, my driving days are over. If I want to go somewhere, I'll rely on my phone. Or my feet, which are now a carbon footprint size smaller."

"So you don't need help unpacking?"

"Already done. But I'm always happy for a visit."

We have croissants and hot chocolate on his balcony. It's a beautiful February day. The fourteenth, I realize, glancing at his classic L.L. Bean watch.

"Happy Valentine's Day, Mr. Kalman."

"Happy Valentine's Day, Sam."

Neither one of us has a sweetheart. His died five years ago, and I'm only twelve.

"Mr. Kalman," I say, "what does it mean to ratify the era?"

"Era, or E.R.A.?"

"I'm not sure. I saw it on a lady's hat just now. In the elevator."

"Probably refers to the Equal Rights Amendment. I've landed in a very political building."

"Equal rights for whom?"

"Women. The ERA was a proposed amendment to the Constitution. Proposed in 1923. Passed by Congress in 1972. Never got the votes to be ratified, though."

"What's it say?"

"'Equality of rights under the law shall not be denied or abridged by the United States or by any state on account of sex.'"

"Isn't that already the law?"

"Nope. There's nothing in the Constitution that guarantees equality for women."

"I thought you said it passed in 1972."

"Passed *Congress* in 1972. An amendment has to then be approved by three-fourths of all the states. A nearly impossible task. By 1977, thirty-five states had ratified. Imagine . . . they needed just three more. Time was running out. The ERA was set to expire in 1979. On the ninth of July, 1978, a hundred thousand people went to Washington. A sea of purple, gold, and white banners — the colors of the suffragist movement — come to demand an extension."

"And?"

"It was a great success. Congress gave the amendment five more years. Five years later, know how many had ratified?"

I shake my head. No idea.

"Still thirty-five. They were three short when the clock ran out. The amendment died."

The way he talks about it sounds as if the amendment wasn't just a piece of paper, but something alive, with hope. Until it died.

Just then it starts to rain. *Drip, drip, drop.* Right onto Mr. Kalman's croissant.

We look up. The water is coming from 403.

"Hey!" Mr. Kalman says. "You're raining on our parade!"

Skateboard Girl pops her head over the rail. Her nana peers down too. "Sorry about that. We're planting seeds."

"All pots must have saucers under them. No dripping allowed. Have you read your lease?"

"She's read the lease," Skateboard Girl says.

"It says no hammering in the halls," Betty calls down.

Oh, boy, I think. His first weekend in the apartment, and Mr. Kalman's already at war.

17
★

Then I notice a missed FaceTime from Alistair, so I call him back.

"Alistair?" I say. "You FaceTimed?"

"You with Mr. Kalman?"

"He's right here. What's wrong?"

"I'm about to get arrested."

"Wait, what? Where are you?"

"Portland, Oregon. I flew up last night to join a group of climate activists. They needed someone to stand on a mound of dirt—a garden, actually—and said it should be a kid. The oil and gas industry is less likely to shoot a kid. I thought about you, Sam, how you stood on the desk that time, so I volunteered."

He flips the camera around, and I see Alistair standing face-to-nose with a huge locomotive, a long line of train cars behind it. All of them have scary stickers that say FLAMMABLE.

Alistair pans down to his feet. He's on top of a dirt pile as high as the locomotive, with plants growing up around him —like Max in *Where the Wild Things Are*.

"Who plants a garden in the middle of train tracks?"

"We did. To stop the train."

He pans to the crowd of protesters holding signs that say FIGHT FOSSIL FUELS; NO TAR SAND OIL IN OUR TOWN; EXTINCTION REBELLION NOW.

"The plan is to obstruct this company because their actions are contributing to climate change. Think I'll make the news?"

"Ye-ah."

"International, I hope. Maybe I'll hear from Greta. Listen, they're coming for me. I've got to sign off, but can you hand the phone to Mr. Kalman?"

I hand the phone to Mr. Kalman.

"Hello, Alistair."

"I called your cell. You didn't pick up."

"Sam was making a terrible racket with the hammer. Looks like you're ready for my services."

"I'll say!" Alistair flips the camera again. A dozen squad cars and a paddy wagon are pulling up to the train.

"Come down from that pile of dirt!" an officer squawks through a bullhorn.

"This isn't a pile of dirt," Alistair says. "It's a garden. And I'm not coming down until that train goes back to the tar sands of Canada and never comes back!"

The crowd cheers, raising fists and signs. I've never seen Alistair so fired up about anything. Not even avocado toast.

On-screen, I see police climbing the hill, closing in.

"Your parents with you, Alistair?"

"Down below, with the protesters."

"Perfect," Mr. Kalman says. "We'll see you soon."

He clicks off and hands me the phone. I look at him, worried.

"They'll take him to a juvenile detention center. He'll have to stay there overnight. With any luck, he'll get a speedy trial."

The doorbell rings.

"Sam, would you mind?" He nods toward the front door.

I go through the apartment and open the door. I can hardly believe it. Catalina and Jaesang walk in wearing black Extinction Rebellion T-shirts.

"What are you guys doing here?"

"Mr. Kalman texted this morning," Jaesang says.

"Said Alistair was going to get arrested. We should come right over," Catalina says.

I turn to Mr. Kalman, furious. "You planned this all along?"

"Let's just say it's a coordinated effort. Alistair told me he felt powerless but wanted to take civic action against global warming. I have some old lefty friends in Oregon who were planning to stop the New Horizon Energy trains from delivering their next load of oil to a refinery. I put one friend together with some others. That's why I told you to get here at ten. The demonstration was scheduled for then, and there's an Alaska Airlines flight at noon. Soon as I got the go-ahead from your parents, I booked us all seats. We're going to Portland as a show of support."

His phone chimes. He looks down at it. "Our Uber is here."

Man, I should've seen this coming.

3

His Own Recognizance

They took Alistair to the Donald E. Long Juvenile Detention Center and booked him on charges of criminal trespassing and obstruction of commerce. The trespassing charge carries a maximum sentence of thirty days in jail. The obstruction of commerce charge carries a maximum sentence of *twenty years*. Since Alistair is under eighteen, Oregon state law says that he gets a trial by a judge, not a jury.

The Donald E. Long Detention Center is only ten minutes from the Portland airport. We Uber straight there, and with every minute that goes by, I feel my stomach twisting tighter and tighter.

Alistair cries over burnt koalas. What's going to happen when he's locked up in juvy? I picture him balled up in the corner of a jail cell, bullies taunting him through the bars. Or worse, in the communal showers, with those same bullies hurling soap turds at his head. And what'll he eat? Nothing he's ever eaten before.

"Mr. Kalman, does he really have to spend the night? Can't we bail him out now?"

"'Fraid not, Sam. In America, juveniles do not have the right to bail."

"Let's bust him out!" Catalina says. Her Extinction Rebellion T-shirt puffs up. Like my mom always says, *Dress the part and you'll find the heart.*

"Too risky. Look, kids. Rules are rules. The Multnomah County legal code expressly states that a minor who is booked for a felony or misdemeanor offense must spend one night in a detention center. We'll try to get him released as soon as possible on his own recognizance."

"What's his own recognizance?" Jaesang asks.

"A legal term that means, instead of posting bail, a defendant makes a promise to appear in court. The judge will make a decision based on Alistair's prior record, his flight risk, and other factors, such as the likelihood that he'll commit another crime while he's out."

"Will it help if we vouch for him?" Jaesang says.

"Another reason you three are here."

• • •

We get to the Long Detention Center around 2:45. The sign is clear: visiting hours Monday through Thursday, 6:00 p.m. to 8:00 p.m. Saturday and Sunday, 12:00–3:00. At the front desk, Mr. Kalman asks to see Alistair's case manager, the state-appointed counselor who oversees his arrest.

Soon a tall woman in a red suit comes to talk to us. She has very high cheekbones and very high hair. She looks like she could be a school principal or a judge, or something in between, which is exactly what she is.

Her badge says MELISSA DUPRE.

"Good afternoon, Ms. Dupre. My name is Avi Kalman. I'm here to see one of your inmates, Alis—"

"Family visits are Monday through Thursday, six p.m. to eight p.m. Saturday and Sunday, twelve to three. No weekend check-ins after two forty-five. And non-eligible visitors—anyone under eighteen—may not wait in the lobby."

We look up at the digital clock on the wall: 2:47.

"Yes, but as his defense attorn—"

"Professional visits are Monday through Friday, nine a.m. to five p.m."

"What about religious visits?"

"Which religion?"

"How about Jewish? It's the Sabbath."

She folds over a few forms on her clipboard. Under religious preference, Alistair checked undecided. (He's Jewish on his mom's side, Episcopalian on his dad's.)

"You'll have to wait until professional visiting hours Monday morning."

We start to leave, but I turn back.

"What'll he eat?" I ask.

Melissa Dupre changes clipboards.

"Saturday dinner . . . pizza with salad, chocolate pudding. Sunday, burritos."

"No vegetables?"

"There's green peppers in the burritos, tomato in the pizza sauce."

"Homemade crust or frozen?"

"I wouldn't know. You can ask him about it during visiting hours. But no visitors under eighteen are permitted inside the building."

How's *that* constitutional?

• • •

We have thirty-six hours in Portland, the City of Roses. Catalina suggests that we visit the arboretum in Washington Park.

"This is a working vacation, kids," Mr. Kalman says. "We have to prepare Alistair's defense."

"Exactly why we should spend time in nature. While there's still nature to spend time in."

We hop on a Max—Portand's light-rail system—toward Washington Park. Hoyt Arboretum is a short walk from the station, and we get there an hour before closing time. The sign by the entrance highlights what to see in winter, but really there's no discussion. We head for the Magnolia Trail.

Magnolia trees have been on Earth for ninety-five million years. Their pink, red, or white flowers can spread up to twelve inches wide. Their wood is soft, so they aren't often cut down. Songbirds love them.

As soon as we're on the trail, everything gets quiet. It's the same cathedral quiet I felt inside the Supreme Court, a silence of awe and respect. There, it was respect for justice, the idea that if you were harmed by a person or a policy, there was a place where you could go for help. Here, it's respect for nature and all the things you notice if you let yourself be quiet long enough to listen, and look.

Like the wind lifting Catalina's hair and letting it fall again. Or the shadow and sunlight taking turns on the sleeve of Mr. Kalman's windbreaker. Or the crunch of Jaesang's Jordans on the gravel path. And the birdsong, a whole concert happening for free.

We sit on a bench under a saucer magnolia, according to its tag. Just sit, breathing the cold, damp air, listening to nature.

I look up and see hundreds of pink buds, like tiny fists, waiting for spring to open them. And then, in a whisper no louder than the wind, Mr. Kalman thanks Catalina for suggesting this place.

"It's everything Alistair is fighting for."

"Why did they pick Portland?" Jaesang asks.

"Here in Oregon, the law permits citizens to take illegal action in order to prevent a worse action from going forward. It's called the necessity defense."

"You mean, you can break the law to save a life?"

"As long as your action is necessary and there's no other way."

"Does the planet count as a life?" I ask.

"That's what we're going to ask the court to decide."

We sit there a moment longer.

"Why *two* nights in jail?" I say.

"Arrested on a Saturday. Courts don't open up 'til Monday."

"Think he'll be okay?"

"He'll be okay," Mr. Kalman says. "But he won't be the same."

• • •

Mr. Kalman loves historic hotels. In Portland the most famous hotel is The Benson. Presidents and prime ministers have stayed there. Elvis Presley stayed there. Mitch Mitchell, Jimi Hendrix's drummer, died there. There was a lion in the lobby once. And in 1993 President Clinton recorded a radio address to the nation from his suite at The Benson.

"You sure we can afford this place?" Jaesang asks.

We look up at the tree-high wedding cake ceilings, dangling, domed chandeliers, and oil paintings of rich people on the walls. There's a gym, but they call it a *fitness facility*.

"My realtor already has multiple offers on my house," Mr. Kalman says. "So let's enjoy ourselves, including room service."

As soon as we check into the junior suite, we pick up the phone. Jaesang orders eggs Benedict, Catalina a crab salad, and Mr. Kalman a Monte Cristo sandwich.

"Sam?"

I look at the menu. Even the font is fancy. The word *sumptuous* comes to mind. But so does Alistair alone in his cell—or worse, with company—staring down a slice of cold pizza. What kind of person feasts on five-star room service while his climate warrior friend is eating jailhouse slop?

"I'll just have cereal," I say. "Box of cornflakes'll be fine."

Jaesang and Cat guess why.

"Yeah, me too," Catalina says. "With half a banana if anyone wants to split one."

"I'll get some oatmeal," Jaesang says.

We have our cornflakes and oatmeal out of porcelain bowls, our milk from a silver pitcher. The banana comes presliced, but at least we've gone modest in Alistair's honor.

Mr. Kalman, on the other hand, is sticking with the Monte Cristo.

4

The Necessity Defense

The Long Detention Center (and I hope it doesn't live up to its name) opens Monday at 9:00 a.m. At 8:45 we're outside. We're missing a day of school for what Mr. Kalman calls a real-world lesson in civics. Ironically, only Mr. Kalman is allowed inside, so Jaesang, Catalina, and I hang back about twenty feet from the door. The mid-February air is cold; a breeze makes it feel colder.

"You guys smell something?" Jaesang says.

"Bacon," I say.

We drift around to the side of the building. About eight feet up from the ground, there's an open window, the source of the scent. Soon we smell eggs and cream and toasting English muffins. All at once our three stomachs rumble and growl like stray dogs about to fight over food. As if all we had for dinner for two nights was cereal, which is exactly what we had for dinner for two nights. The scent grows richer, creamier, until I think I know what it is. Can it be—eggs Benedict?

"Guys, give me a boost."

Jaesang braids his fingers for the first step; Catalina, who's taller, braids hers for the second; and I parkour off his shoulder and onto hers until I'm high enough look in through the window.

I'm expecting to see a crew of cooks in hairnets, but what I see instead is—

"Alistair?"

"Sam!"

He comes to the window dressed not in prison orange but in chef's white—the shirt *and* the tall hat.

"What are you doing in the kitchen?" I ask.

"Cooking, what else?"

"But . . . aren't you supposed to be in jail?"

"The Long Detention Center has a cooking school for kids in juvy. It's useful job training for when they come out. Someone on staff recognized me from *MasterChef Junior.* They asked if I'd like to teach a breakfast class."

He turns, looks over his shoulder. "Riley, you want to bring the béchamel down to a simmer. Too high and it'll get too thick."

He turns back to the window.

"Riley's in for grand theft scooter. She'll make a great chef someday."

"Alistair, we were so worried about you. Know what we had for dinner all weekend?"

"Where'd you stay?"

"The Benson."

"They have a four-star chef. I hope you ordered seafood."

"Cereal. In solidarity with you."

"I would have had the scallops." He pokes his head out and looks down at Catalina and Jaesang. "Hi, guys. Wow, it's good to see you."

"We got you a present," I say, holding up a bag from Powell's Books, where we spent a few hours on Sunday.

Alistair opens it. *Recipes of Sweden: A Classic Swedish Cookbook* by Inga Norberg.

"Thanks, guys. I don't have this one."

"Are you okay?" Jaesang asks.

"I am, yeah. Prison has given me a whole new perspective. I feel less afraid than I was before. And ready for the fight ahead."

"That really smells good," Catalina says.

"Too bad they don't allow visitors under eighteen," Jaesang says.

Finally, the color orange comes into view. Riley's hair. Through the bars of the window she hands me a paper towel with some food on it. The creamy, cheesy, toasty scent of three eggs Benedict nearly knocks me off Catalina's shoulders.

"That's *meatless* eggs Benedict," Alistair says. "I used Canadian fakin' in Greta's honor."

I hand our breakfast down to Jaesang and parkour back to the ground. We huddle together, eating a gourmet breakfast made by our jailbird friend.

• • •

At two p.m. we meet up with Alistair's parents at the Multnomah County Courthouse. Mr. Kalman filed a motion to have Alistair's case dismissed, but the district attorney, a blond-haired woman in a crisp blue dress, has something else in mind.

"Your Honor, this twelve-year-old boy disrupted the supply chain in an industry vital to the state of Oregon. If we allow these so-called climate warriors to use terrorist tactics against the fossil fuel industry, the economic toll will be devastating. The loss could be as high as twenty-seven percent of the state's corporate tax revenue. That's money gone from schools, libraries, streets, first responders, and, of course, your salary. The DA's office would like to see you make an example of the boy's behavior."

"What do you recommend?"

"Under Section 1951 of the U.S. Criminal Code, the maximum penalty for willful interference of commerce is twenty years. He's a minor, so I think it would be appropriate to impose ten percent of the maximum penalty."

Alistair jumps up. "Two years? You're going to make me go through puberty in prison?"

The judge slams her gavel onto shiny wood. Alistair sits back down.

"Defense?"

Mr. Kalman rises.

"Your Honor, my client was exercising his right under Oregon state law to use any means necessary to right a wrong. His actions, though illegal, were necessary to stop the dangerous and destructive practice of transporting raw oil shale through the city. Those train tracks pass within a thousand feet of people's homes. Those people may be poor, but they have a right to breathe clean air."

"In order to persuade me with the necessity defense, you have to prove that your client exhausted all other avenues of protest."

"Our people tried picketing," Alistair says. "They spoke at city hall. What did that get us? Bupkes—"

The DA interrupts. "This boy is a child being used by adults to carry out their political agenda. If you don't punish him, other minors will be exploited in the same way."

"Listen, lady," Alistair says, rising again, "nobody's manipulating me. I stood on that mound of soil because I wanted to. I stopped that train because I had to. I may be a prepu ... prepubes ... just a kid, but that doesn't mean I can't think for myself. Judge, if you believe I broke the law, then sentence me. But keep in mind, sometimes two wrongs *do* make a right. Sometimes, it's the only way."

I wish we weren't bound by the courtroom code of silence, because right now I'd like to jump up and shout *Go, Alistair!* and leap onto his shoulders. But I restrain myself and make a secret, triumphant fist in my seat.

The judge looks at the DA.

She looks at Mr. Kalman.

Then she looks at Alistair, who looks right back.

And doesn't look away.

It's a staring contest between Alistair and the judge.

"You want me to punish you?" she says.

"If you believe what I did was wrong, yes."

She turns to Mr. Kalman. "You want me to dismiss the charges?"

"Under Oregon's necessity defense, yes."

She turns to the DA. "You want me to impose a sentence?"

"It would send the right message, Your Honor."

There's this long, terrifying pause. As clean and fresh as the air was under the magnolia tree, that's how thick and heavy it feels in here.

Finally, the judge speaks.

"I'm going to give the kid what he wants," she says. "In the matter of *Multnomah County v. Alistair Martin*, a minor charged with unlawful trespassing and interference with commerce, I pronounce you guilty as charged."

Alistair's mom and dad hold hands. Jaesang, Catalina, and me all gasp. But Alistair holds it together, stays on his feet.

"And I'm going to give the DA what she wants."

"What's my sentence?" Alistair asks.

"Time served."

The DA can hardly believe her ears. "But that's just two days."

"And during those two days, according to his case officer, he was a model prisoner—both in and out of the kitchen. Keep fighting, Mr. Martin. In the words of a great man—whose first name matches *your* surname—'the arc of the moral universe is long, but it bends toward justice.'"

The gavel comes down.

"Whew," Alistair says. "For a second I thought I'd I have to be bar mitzvahed behind bars."

• • •

Outside the courthouse, we gather on the steps, and now I can give Alistair the bear hug I've been saving.

But Jaesang is, well, a little bit somber.

"Don't know why you're celebrating. Now he's got a record."

"It'll be expunged when he turns eighteen," Mr. Kalman says.

"Besides, he's in good company," Catalina says. "Rosa Parks. Gandhi. Martin Luther King. Cesar Chavez. Lots of famous activists have been arrested."

A reporter from a local news channel puts a fuzzy microphone in front of Alistair. A cameraman points a fat lens at him. Alistair soaks up the attention like someone who's been on TV before.

That's because he's been on TV before.

He starts praising his defense attorney —

"Come here, Mr. Kalman, get in the shot."

He starts praising his support team —

"You guys, too."

And he says he has a warning for the fossil fuel industry. "This isn't over, polluters!"

A big crowd has gathered, and a woman steps forward and asks if she can speak to Alistair. Kids trail her — from really short kindergartners to hairy-faced high school students. She introduces herself as Julia Olson, the chief legal counsel for Our Children's Trust.

"We're an organization out of Eugene," she says. "We brought a class action lawsuit against the United States government for its policies that are contributing to climate change."

"I heard about you guys," I say. "*Juliana v. United States.* You lost at the Ninth Circuit Court of Appeals."

"We did, yes." She looks at me. "You're Sam, aren't you? Sam Warren?"

"Yeah."

"We followed your case against homework. You're a hero to a lot of kids."

I look at all the kids standing with her. I look at Alistair and think, a lot of kids are heroes to me.

"You know, Ms. Olson," I say. "The judge inside, she told Alistair to keep fighting. Same goes for you. Don't you have one last appeal — to the U.S. Supreme Court?"

"We filed an appeal six months ago, Sam. Their silence means they probably won't hear our case."

I look at Alistair, who nods. We look at Jaesang and Catalina, who nod. We all look at Mr. Kalman, who shrugs.

"We can help," I say.

I pull out my cell phone and make a call. She answers right

away. That's the thing about my big sister. She always answers right away.

"Sadie," I say, "how would you like to take a little time off from college?"

5

The Lounge War

Last year, when we sued to stop homework, Mr. Kalman was our coach, but Sadie was the captain of our team. Sadie knew how to turn anger into action. Sadie had the guts to argue in front of the scary justices of the Supreme Court.

She was also my personal champion. All my life, when I'd feel anxious, Sadie would help me feel calm. When I'd feel small, she'd lower the world for me.

She'd also lower the Nerf hoop so I could dunk. Basically, she's the best big sister you could ask for. So, when I tell her we need her help to convince the Supreme Court that they *have to* take *Juliana* on appeal, I'm feeling really strong, really tall.

And the last thing I'm expecting her to say is "Sorry, Sam, I can't."

"What do you mean, you can't?"

"I have two papers due next week and a debate tournament

next month. If we win, we qualify for nationals. And I just got an internship doing outreach with homeless women in Providence."

"But you already proved you're the best debater in the world. You got homework kicked out of school."

"Middle school. And high school. College is different."

"How so?"

"This is work I want to do, Sam."

I don't know what to say, so I don't say anything. The silence swallows us both.

"Sam? You okay?"

"This fight—against the government, to save the planet—it's so much bigger than the last one. We can't do it without you."

"Yes, you can, Sam. I have faith in you. Listen, I gotta go. I'm late for a study session."

And just like that, my big sister ditches me.

• • •

On the Saturday after we sprung—sprang?—Alistair from juvy, we meet up in the lounge of the NoHo Senior Arts Colony. Mr. Kalman said that his 643-square-foot apartment was suitable for one man in his ninth decade, but not for the whole team. The lounge, on the other hand, has a pool table, a flat-screen TV, a sectional couch, and a small communal kitchen with a microwave and a mini-fridge.

41
★

We turn the pool table into our conference table, and we all sit around and plan our strategy to get the Supreme Court to take the climate change lawsuit on appeal.

"There's never been a case like *Juliana v. United States,*" Mr. Kalman begins. "Like our case against the school board, theirs is a class action lawsuit brought by kids, but they're suing the whole U.S. government. Their claim? The government looks the other way while oil and gas companies wreck the environment. And kids suffer the most because you're facing a future of rising sea levels, raging forest fires, mass migration, and mass extinction."

"Where's the constitutional violation?" Catalina asks. For a case to win at the Supreme Court, it has to have a reason to be there.

"The Fifth Amendment says the government can't take away your life, liberty, or property without due process," Jaesang says. "By failing to protect the environment, they're violating the Fifth. Should be a slam dunk case."

"Well, Jaesang," Mr. Kalman says, "the problem with *Juliana,* according to a three-judge panel on the Ninth Circuit Court of Appeals, is that they're asking courts to take *a priori* action to stop a coming threat. To prove standing in a lawsuit, you have to show *a posteriori* damages."

This is when I need my big sister to translate into Little Brother English.

"I don't get it," I say.

From across the room a voice calls out, "He said you can't sue someone until after they've hurt you."

It's Skateboard Girl. She must visit her grandma every Saturday. She rolls up to us and says, "He used the Latin legal terms for *before* and *after*."

"What grade are you even in?" Jaesang asks.

"Seventh."

"What's your name?"

"Zoe."

"Where do you go to school, Zoe?"

"Right here."

We look around. I don't know many classrooms with a pool table, a flat-screen TV, and a mini-fridge.

"In a senior living complex? I thought you had to be, like, over seventy-five to live here."

"Sixty-two. But in my case, the board made an exception. Can I turn on the TV? It's relevant to your cause."

Zoe steps to the TV, grabs the remote, and turns on Netflix. She keeps the volume low, but soon I hear this British man talking about our planet. I look over and see that first-ever photograph of Earth taken from space. It was in 1968, when the *Apollo* astronauts looked back at a blue marble floating in a sea of black. Our planet, suspended in space.

The British guy narrates: "Our home was not limitless. There was an edge to our existence. It was a rediscovery of a fundamental truth. We are ultimately bound by and reliant upon the finite natural world . . ."

And then, in a quiet voice, Catalina says, "It isn't *a priori.*"

We all look at her.

"My sister was traumatized by the jet fuel they dumped on her," she says. "And kids in my neighborhood, they have high rates of asthma because the air is so bad. My abuelita suffers too."

"Since the California wildfires," Jaesang adds, "hardly any birds come to our backyard feeder anymore. Me and my grandfather are keeping track."

Jaesang's other obsession, besides the weather, is birds. He and his grandpa take pictures of them with his grandpa's Pentax. And every year they join in the Great Backyard Bird Count. He says you can track climate change by paying attention to birds.

"James gets all lethargic when it's over ninety degrees," Alistair says. "He stays in his rosemary burrow. He won't even eat escarole. We've had seventeen days over ninety degrees so far this year."

Alistair loves James, his tortoise. He named him after another of his favorite chefs, James Beard.

On-screen, the British man tells us that over the last hundred years, more than five hundred species have gone extinct. Without humans, that number would be under twenty.

"Three things we have to know more about," Mr. Kalman says. "Legal precedents. Damages to the environment. Damages to living things. Now partner up and get to work."

We don't get far before Zoe's grandma comes into the lounge, along with five other residents. The sight of Mr. Kalman and a bunch of kids spread out around the pool table makes them all hit the brakes on their walkers.

"The lounge is reserved for Memoir Writing Group from ten to eleven on Saturday mornings," Grandma Betty says.

"There was no mention of that in my lease," Mr. Kalman says.

"It's posted outside the door."

Betty nods toward the hall, where a sign says, LOUNGE RESERVED SATURDAYS 10–11 A.M. FOR MEMOIR GROUP.

Mr. Kalman shrugs, takes a Sharpie from his pencil case, and starts writing on his yellow legal pad. He tears off the paper and turns to Catalina.

"Anybody got tape?"

Catalina hands him some.

Mr. Kalman gets up, crosses the lounge, and posts a new sign next to the old: LOUNGE RESERVED SATURDAYS 10–11 A.M. FOR LEGAL CONFERENCE.

45

★

"There," he says, "now we've both got signs."

"You can't just add a sign," Betty says.

"It's a First Amendment right."

"I'll be taking this up with the board," she says.

At the mention of the word *board,* I start to worry. Ever since he was a kid, Mr. Kalman has been . . . what's the word . . . pugilistic? Pugnacious? Defiant? Well, I learned a lot of synonyms for what Mr. Kalman has been. At eleven he took on Big Joe Mancuso, the Brooklyn bully who pinned him to the ground. Mr. Kalman never said uncle, and he got Big Joe Mancuso to cry. At ninety, he took on the Los Angeles Unified School District. And in between, he took on just about anyone who tried to pick on kids.

But I'm not sure this is a good fight for him. He just moved in, after all. He deserves a little peace in his old age.

That's when the idea hits me. The perfect way to get Mr. Kalman and Betty to get along.

"Hey, Zoe," I say. "Want to help us save the planet?"

6

We Build a Case

When we break into teams, it's a little awkward because Zoe says, "I'll work with Sam."

And Catalina says, "I thought I was working with Sam."

"I thought you were working with Jaesang," I say.

"Jaesang is working with Alistair," Catalina says, "on animals. Me and Sam are working on precedents."

"Who're you working with, Mr. Kalman?"

"I like to work alone."

"Me too," I say, even though I really don't. "I'll work on case histories."

"But that's the same thing as precedents," Catalina says.

"Why don't you both work with Sam?" Mr. Kalman says. And he *winks* at me. Really, Mr. Kalman.

So now I'm working with two girls on case studies and precedents, which is two different ways of saying the same thing.

But I'm not distracted, even though Zoe has this maze of

freckles on her nose and I imagine playing Dot to Dot with them. I draw them one way and get the constellation Orion. Draw them another and I get the bear. Backwards and I see a boat. At the same time, I'm paying attention to what Catalina is reading off her laptop, about a guy whose pigs stank and his neighbor sued him. And I'm paying attention to Catalina's eyes bouncing between her laptop screen and my face, and her long strand of hair that's not in a braid anymore but falling down her shoulder like a stream.

Wait, what's the matter with me? I used to be good at concentrating.

We work for a while, snack for a while, work some more. I notice Jaesang and Alistair wincing at some photos on the internet. "No way, we can't show them *that*," Jaesang says. And Alistair says, "We have to, Jae. We have to show the truth."

For lunch, Alistair makes Mr. Kalman's tuna salad sandwiches on toasted egg bread, and when he delivers a round to the Memoir Writing Group over by the big-screen TV, I see Zoe's grandma take a bite and smile.

"*You* made these?" she says to Alistair.

"Mr. Kalman's recipe," he says.

She looks across the lounge at Mr. Kalman. Her eyebrows go up like they're on tippy-toes.

• • •

48
★

After lunch we group up around the pool table/conference table. Alistair and Jaesang go first.

I know I should keep my eyes shut. I don't need to look to know that humans have done terrible things to our animal friends. If I look, I'll have nightmares and lose a ton of sleep. Like my mom always says, *Sleep or weep*.

But maybe we *should* weep. If we look away, nothing will change.

I open my eyes.

There's a picture of the cutest little sea lion—whiskers wide around his snout, eyes glossy black, wet nose all shiny.

His head is wrapped in white gauze. Thin plastic tubes stick out from his neck.

"This little guy had epilepsy caused by brain cancer," Alistair explains. "He ate toxins from a chemical dumpsite in the Pacific Ocean. Divers found him twitching in the water. They got him up to the surface, took him to a vet who did brain surgery on him. They saved his life, but there were many more like him they couldn't save."

Alistair adds, "And look at this."

The next slide shows a big dog—maybe an Irish wolfhound—that's lost of lot of weight. But I look closer and see that it's not a dog, but a polar bear standing on a tiny wedge of ice. He looks frightened. All around him there's water, but no ice, no land.

"As the polar ice caps disappear, the bears can't find enough food. Scientists predict that if we don't stop the warming of the planet, polar bears will go extinct by 2100."

Another slide shows a frightened baby orangutan. Behind him, a whole forest of trees lies flat on the ground.

"His family lived in those trees," Alistair says. "In their natural state, the tropical forests weren't making enough money, so the governments of Malaysia and Indonesia let farmers cut them down. They turned a natural ecosystem into a palm oil farm. You guys probably don't know this, but palm oil is in all kinds of foods that you eat. Every bite of Nutella is potentially a dead ape. Jae."

They switch places, and we see pictures of Jaesang's backyard under an orange sky.

"When California, Oregon, and Washington were on fire —three million acres burned—remember the smoke cloud over the city? Birds stopped coming to our feeders. They were hiding in their nests. Birds are like a barometer for climate change. They tell us how healthy the planet is. Since 1970, in the U.S. alone, we've lost more than three *billion* birds. Half the population of seabirds is gone. And it's only getting worse."

Jaesang shows the picture of a beach on St. Paul Island, rows of dead puffins on the sand.

"Almost three hundred dead puffins washed up on this island between Alaska and Russia. Stormier seas. Warmer water. More dead birds . . . Climate change."

Mr. Kalman turns toward us.

"Sam, Zoe, Catalina, how can the law help?"

"The first case about the environment," Zoe says, "was a fight over pigs. It was way back in 1516 in England. This guy with an apple orchard thought he could make more money selling pork than fruit, so he turned his orchard into a pig farm. His neighbor liked the sweet smell of apple blossoms near their common fence but was surprised one day by a new smell: swine poop. He complained. His neighbor said, 'You don't like my pigsty, move. It's my land, and I can do whatever I want.'"

"They took their case to the King's Bench," Catalina says. "That's what the British called court back then. Know what the judge said?"

She pauses for dramatic effect. "Sam, tell them."

Sometimes Catalina twists that strand of hair and tosses it back over her shoulder. And sometimes her timing is terrible because she does it when I'm supposed to be listening to something important.

"Sam?"

"The king said . . . what did the king say again?"

Zoe sighs. "*Publicum bonum privato est praeferendum.* The public good over the private. It means you can't wreck your neighbor's air or their view."

Then Catalina says, "This is, like, the biggest idea in environmental law. Public good over the private, right? So you'd expect all the environmental cases that follow to protect the people and the planet we live on. Tell them about Lujan, Sam."

Lujan? Chevron? I should never have worked with girls.

"I'll let Zoe tell."

She tells them about this case, but I only catch about every fifth word. *Endangered. Nixon. Crocodile. Wildlife.* She's got this look in her eyes . . . confidence mixed with anger. It makes you feel safe around her. Like she'll stand up for what's right.

"In *Lujan v. Defenders of Wildlife,* the lower courts agreed with the wildlife defenders," Zoe says. "Manuel Lujan appealed to the Supreme Court."

"And?"

"The Supreme Court ruled. In a six to three decision *against* Kelly and the crocodiles, they said she didn't have standing to sue because she didn't show that actual harm was done to her. 'A risk to animals,' Lujan's lawyer said, 'does not translate into injury to a human being.'"

"What about injury to the planet itself?" Alistair says. "Isn't Earth an endangered species?"

"Good question, Alistair," Catalina says. "In *Sierra Club v. Morton,* Disney wanted to build an eighty-acre ski area in Sequoia National Forest. They found the perfect spot, but they'd have to build a highway and power lines through the forest. The Sierra Club sued to the stop the development. The Supreme Court said the Sierra Club didn't have standing. Know why?"

They all shake their heads, except for Mr. Kalman. He knows why, but he lets Catalina explain.

"No one in the Sierra Club actually lived in the Sequoia National Forest. No harm to people, no case."

"If the defenders of wildlife couldn't save the crocodile," I say, "and the Sierra Club couldn't save the Sequoias, how are we going to save the planet?"

"We have to prove imminent harm," Mr. Kalman says, "not just to all children, but to particular children. To you."

It gets quiet in the NoHo Senior Arts lounge. You can hear all five of us kids thinking. We care about the planet, of course, in a general *I love the animals and trees* kind of way. But it's so much bigger than that. If humans keep warming the atmosphere, it's not just a few species that will die; it's all of us. Our future literally depends on it.

"We are being harmed. Right now," Catalina says. We all look at her. "When they dumped jet fuel on my sister, that was a direct harm."

"One plane, Catalina. One mistake. We're taking on the whole industry and the government that supports it."

"Wait, Mr. Kalman . . ." Zoe says. "I read the transcript of the *Juliana* case. They did show standing. One kid got sick from breathing polluted air after Oregon's wildfires. Another had his house ruined by sewage after a hurricane in Louisiana. And what Catalina just said, about her neighborhood suffering a worse impact. Why didn't the plane dump fuel on a *different* part of the city? On Beverly Hills or Bel Air?"

"Those neighborhoods weren't in its flight plan."

"Planes never fly over rich people's homes. Plus, there are more trees in those parts of town. Better air quality. If we can show that climate change is harder on the poor—and our government is at fault for letting big companies pollute—then they're in violation of the Fourteenth Amendment: equal protection under the law."

"I like your thinking, Zoe," says Mr. Kalman. "It's bold. And it might persuade the justices. But so far they've refused to take the case."

"Can I show one more picture?" Alistair says.

He spins his laptop around and shows us a selfie of him at the Griffith Park Observatory.

Catalina gives him a look. "Haven't you had enough fame on TV?"

"It's not me I want you to look at. It's the city. The sky."

Behind him, all of Los Angeles is spread out under a sparkling blue sky, with pure white puffball clouds.

"Know when this picture was taken?" he says.

We shake our heads.

"During the COVID lockdown. Everyone stayed home for two weeks. No cars on the freeways. No ships in port. No buses on the road. For two weeks the city shut down, and this is what it looked like. Wild animals came down from the hills. Birds flew back to branches. From downtown, you could see the ocean. From the Santa Monica Pier, you could see Catalina Island. It's like what the British guy was saying in that documentary. If we change our ways, there's hope for the planet to heal. If we can just get in front of the justices, we can convince them to hear our case. I know we can."

"I can get us there," Jaesang says. And we all look at him —like, how?

7

We Zoombomb the
Supreme Court

There's probably a law that says you can't Zoombomb the Supreme Court. But, as Alistair proved, sometimes you have to break the law for the right cause. And if you know someone who knows someone who knows someone who knows the access code, you can break into a telephone conference call of the Supreme Court.

Jaesang's cousin is a computer science major at Stanford. She's doing an internship at IBM and has access to Watson, their supercomputer. As a favor to Jaesang, she used it to hack the federal government's SOCA — secure online conferencing application. It's basically Zoom for the government.

On Monday, before school, we're back in the lounge with our computers ready. Even Betty, who self-identifies as a Supreme Court junkie, woke up early for this. It's 6:30 West Coast time, 9:30 for the justices of the Supreme Court. They're in their pre-arguments morning meeting, a Monday tradition where they talk about the week of cases ahead.

Alistair is in the kitchenette whipping up hot chocolate. At 6:45 we get a text from Jaesang's cousin with the log-in and password.

At 6:50 we log on to the meeting.

You'd expect the nine justices of the Supreme Court to be discussing important legal matters during their Monday morning conference call. Turns out they're talking about the most recent episode of *Saturday Night Live*.

"She had me down to a *T*," says Justice Johnson, the newest member of the court.

"I don't like how Matt Damon does my hair," says Justice Kalvin.

"Sorry to barge in like this, Justices, but we have something more important to talk about than *Saturday Night Live*."

"Alistair?" Chief Justice Reynolds says.

"Hello, Chief! . . . Guys, he remembers me."

"Why are you violating the Computer Fraud and Abuse Act?"

"Please don't press charges. I've already been in juvy once this year for disruption of interstate commerce. Thing is, we need thirty minutes of your time. We're worried about the survival of humans on Earth. We want to help the kids who are suing the federal government over climate change. You heard about their case, right?"

"*Juliana v. United States.* Yes, we know about the case."

"Well, they're dead in the Ninth Circuit. The three-judge panel let stand the lower court's ruling, which said, basically, you can't sue the federal government over what *might* happen."

"That would be an *a priori* judgment, Alistair. You have to prove damages already done."

"We think we can, Chief. We'd like a chance to try."

The line goes quiet. I'm expecting the FBI to burst into the lounge at the NoHo Senior Arts Colony. But the silence is just the chief, thinking.

"Let me put it to my colleagues. Justices, should we take *Juliana* on appeal?"

"If it means bringing back the kids who sued to stop homework," Justice Rauch says, "I say sure. I enjoyed that case."

"I have enough kids at home," Justice Barnett says. "Not sure I want to see a bunch at work."

"But we're fighting for your kids' future, Justice Barnett," Alistair says. "How about you take a vote? All those in favor of hearing the case, raise your blue hand in the chat."

There are nine justices on the call. We need five to get a hearing. The first one up is from Justice Cohen.

One more: Justice Suerte. Catalina smiles. Her favorite Supreme Court justice wants us back.

When we were doing our research for *Warren v. L.A. Unified School District,* we came across a quote from Justice Rauch: "There's no place closer to God than a trout stream."

Sure enough, Justice Rauch's blue hand comes up.

So does Justice Johnson's.

"How about you, Justice DeFazio? Didn't you say that whenever fundamental rights are restricted, the Supreme Court and others cannot close their eyes?"

"That was a case about religious freedom. Don't quote me out of context."

We wait. And wait. We're one hand short.

"Looks like you'll have to grow up and run for Congress, kids," Justice Kalvin says.

"Alistair," Zoe says. "The picture."

"Which one? The sea lion? The orangutan?"

"No! The city."

"Chief, can I share screen?"

"Go ahead."

Alistair shares the picture of Los Angeles on that March day when nature was reborn. "This is our city, Chief, at its best. The air was so clean you could see from the San Bernardino Mountains all the way to the sea. Mornings were full of birdsong.

Afternoons free of smog. The night sky showed off its stars. Know when it was taken? When the pandemic forced us all to stay home for two weeks. Humans stayed in their dens, left their cars in the garage, and Mother Nature had the city to herself again. She healed."

"Alistair, I don't know if the courts are the place to—"

"Please, Chief. Give us a hearing. The whole world will listen."

We have four blue hands. We stare at the screen and pray for just one more.

Prayers can lift you up. Prayers can give you hope.

But sometimes prayers let you down.

"I'm sorry, kids," the chief finally says. "There's nothing in the Constitution that guarantees citizens the right to a stable climate. We're letting the lower court's ruling stand."

8

Nobody Wants Snacks

I haven't seen Alistair this depressed since Anthony Bourdain died. Or Jaesang this depressed since Kobe died. Or Catalina this depressed since her sister got skunked by a jumbo jet. And me? I haven't felt this depressed since my mom lost her job and it was my fault.

The only person who doesn't seem depressed is Mr. Kalman.

"Mr. Kalman," I say a few minutes after we logged off of Zoom, "you seem — I don't know — happy. Are you happy, Mr. Kalman?"

"I'm alive, Sam. At my age, every day the eyes open is a day to rejoice."

"What about the planet? The Supreme Court refused to take the case."

"I told you once, it's their prerogative to hear a case or to pass. But were you listening to what they said?"

"To every word."

"Carefully?"

"Justice Kalvin told us to grow up and vote. Justice DeFazio said don't quote him out of context. Justice Barnett said she's got a lot of kids at home. And the chief said there's nothing in the Constitution that guarantees the right to a stable climate, so they're letting the lower court's ruling stand."

"You did listen. Good. Well, I'm off to Starbucks for coffee and snacks. Alistair, want to come see what's on offer?"

"No, thanks. Not hungry."

"Jaesang, Sam, Zoe?"

"No, thanks," we all say. "Not hungry."

"Wow. You kids *are* depressed. Betty, would you like to get some exercise? A walk'll lift your spirits."

"Who says my spirits need a lift?"

"After all those trips down memory lane with your writing group, I thought—"

"You thought I'd want to take a stroll with a cantankerous old man who's only cheerful when the rest of us are feeling down? I'll stay here with the kids, thank you. But I wouldn't say no to a cup of a coffee. Black with one Sweet'N Low."

"I'll bring you some chocolate-covered graham crackers too. Chocolate-covered graham crackers will cheer everyone up."

For a while we just sit around and stare. The sun is glowing on Catalina's right cheek. In a half hour we have to leave for school.

"This is all my fault," Alistair says. "I wasn't convincing enough."

"It's my fault," I say. "I couldn't get Sadie to help."

"We should've shown them more slides," Jaesang says.

"Guys," Zoe says, "Clarence Darrow, Thurgood Marshall, even RBG wouldn't have persuaded them. There's nothing in the Constitution that can save the planet."

We sit around sulking. Sometimes when you feel really bad, it feels good to sulk.

"If I grow up," Alistair finally says, "I'm going off the grid. I'll live in an Earthship—these totally sustainable homes built into the ground. They're like Hobbit houses. Made from old tires and beer cans and dirt. Solar-powered and self-contained. Even poop gets turned into soil for plants."

"Did you say *if I grow up*?" Betty asks.

"With global warming out of control, I might not make it to thirty."

"Hey," I say, "where's the kid who stopped a train?"

He shrugs.

He shrugs, and I think.

Last year when we took our homework case to the Supreme Court, we made a lot of convincing arguments. Homework takes away the right to privacy (Fourth Amendment). Some kids get help from tutors, but others don't, so it violates the Equal Protection Clause (Fourteenth Amendment).

All our best arguments stood on amendments to the Constitution.

Betty is sitting across the room. She's wearing her favorite baseball cap. I look at it, reading the words over and over again. RATIFY THE ERA.

"That must be a really old hat, Betty," I say.

"It's brand-new. I ordered it online this year."

"I thought it was from your marching days. Mr. Kalman said you were an activist back in the seventies."

"Once an activist, always an activist, Sam. You have to keep fighting for what's right. There's still hope for the ERA, even though the amendment expired."

I keep on staring at her hat. It's like the words are in neon, the way it lights up in my head. Especially the word *ratify*. And as the light pours into the lounge at the NoHo Senior Arts Colony, I start to get an idea. A crazy, they'll-all-probably-laugh-at-me idea. But it's so bright I can't let it go.

"In 1789," I say, "was there anything in the Constitution that gave citizens freedom of religion?"

"No," Catalina says. "That came later, with the Bill of Rights."

"And in 1864, was there anything in the Constitution that outlawed slavery?"

"No," Jaesang says. "Not until the Thirteenth Amendment."

"And in 1918, was there anything in the Constitution that gave women the right to vote?"

"No," Zoe says. "It took the Nineteenth Amendment to give them that right."

"There's nothing in the Constitution that guarantees the right to a safe planet. But what if there was?"

Jaesang, Alistair, Catalina, and Zoe just look at me, confused.

But Betty smiles. She points to her cap.

"They added amendments in the past," I say. "Why not add one now?"

"Because it's practically impossible," Zoe says. "The country is way too divided."

"Impossible?" Jaesang says. "Tell that to Tom Brady, who won his seventh Super Bowl at forty-three years old. Tell it to NASA, who put a rover on Mars. Or to the scientists who made a COVID vaccine in six months."

"Yeah, but the odds —"

"When have we ever cared about the odds?"

"How do you amend the Constitution anyway?" Alistair asks.

"With justice on your side," Betty says. "That's how."

"I mean practically. Like, how does it happen?"

"By putting one foot in front of the other. That's what we did in the seventies. We marched."

"Nana," Zoe says, "when these guys ask a question like how do we amend the Constitution, they're not talking about it in the abstract. They mean, literally, how can we?"

"Oh. You know, I don't know? Better ask Google."

"Okay, Google," Jaesang says into his phone. "How do you amend the Constitution?"

Under Article Five of the Constitution, there are two ways to propose and ratify amendments. To propose amendments, two-thirds of both houses of Congress can vote to propose an amendment, or two-thirds of the state legislatures can ask Congress to call a national convention to propose amendments. Once an amendment is proposed, it must be ratified by three-fourths of the state legislatures in order to become part of the Constitution.

"What's three-fourths of fifty states?"

"Three-fourths of fifty is thirty-seven and a half, so it would take thirty-eight states to ratify an amendment," Catalina says.

"You did that without a calculator?"

"The math is easy, Sam. Getting Congress to pass an amendment—and getting thirty-eight states to sign on—that's going to be hard."

"Which is why you march," Betty says. "But first you have to write."

She gets up from the memoir writing side of the room and comes over to the legal side.

• • •

Jaesang has his laptop open. Betty asks us to say out loud what we're fighting for.

We all start talking at once in this crazy jumble of words, like somebody bumped a Scrabble board.

"Planetclimatesurvivalkoalaspuffinsfoodanimalsairwaterreefsrightbreathecleanpeople."

"Time out, and one at a time," Betty says. "Alistair, what are we fighting for?"

"Survival."

"Survival of who? Survival of what?"

"Us."

"Not just us," Zoe says. "All living things."

"Okay, how do we get there?"

"We have to heal the planet," Jacsang says.

"We have to stop global warming," Catalina says.

"We have to be able to breathe clean air," Zoe says.

"And drink safe water," I say.

"And grow healthy food," Alistair says.

"So let's start with the climate. It has to be, what, steady?"

"How about stable?" Jaesang suggests.

"I like stable. You guys like stable?"

We all nod.

"Okay. *A stable climate being helpful*—"

"Necessary," Zoe says. "That's a very Bill of Rights word."

"*A steady climate being necessary*—"

"For?"

"For the safety?"

"Survival."

"Survival is good. *A stable climate being necessary for the survival of humankind* . . ."

"You're going to leave out animals?"

We all look at Zoe. There's no way we're leaving out animals.

"Life on Earth," I say.

Everyone nods.

"*A stable climate being necessary for the survival of life on Earth* . . ."

"The right of . . . Let's go big. Let's go bold."

"The right of the planet—"

"To be safe—free."

"Free is better."

"Free from what?"

"Pollution."

"Warming."

"Yeah. Unnatural warming."

"Okay. *The right of the planet to be free from pollution and unnatural warming—*"

All together we say, "Shall not be infringed!"

• • •

By the time Mr. Kalman gets back from Starbucks with coffee and chocolate-covered graham crackers, we've written our draft of the Planet Amendment.

"Hey, Mr. Kalman," Alistair says, "we want to read you something."

"You're going to love this, Mr. Kalman," Jaesang says.

"It'll keep you alive for at least another year," I say. "Maybe seven more."

"I'm glad to see everyone's mood has improved."

"Have a seat. Zoe and Catalina will read it to you."

Mr. Kalman shrugs, steps over me, and sits down.

"Ready?"

"Sure."

"*A stable climate being necessary for the survival of life on Earth . . .*" Zoe says.

And then Catalina says, "*. . . the right of the planet to be free from pollution and unnatural warming shall not be infringed.*"

"What is that?"

"Our Planet Amendment to the Constitution. Betty helped us write it."

He looks at Betty, who pumps a fist in the air. Then he looks at us. "Do you know what it takes to amend the Constitution?"

"Three-fourths of the state legislatures."

"That means not just California, Oregon, Washington, and New York. But states like Wyoming, Georgia, West Virginia, and Texas."

"We know the coal states, Mr. Kalman. We know where the pipelines run."

"A Planet Amendment would put the fossil fuel industry out of business."

"And save the planet."

"It would make plastic illegal."

"And save the planet."

"It would make eating meat a crime."

"And save the planet!"

"People could no longer fly in planes."

"In electric ones they could."

"They couldn't have fireworks on the Fourth of July."

"They'll have a light show instead."

"The world isn't ready, kids."

"The world doesn't have a choice," I say. "If we don't do this—and get other countries to follow—our kids won't have a planet to be born on."

He looks at us one by one. He opens a pack of graham

crackers and crunches one. He blows on his coffee, takes a careful sip.

"We'd better book some tickets, then."

"Where to, Mr. Kalman?"

"Washington, D.C."

"What's in D.C.?"

"A hard road ahead."

9

Alistair Writes a Love Letter, and I Get Taller, I Guess

Dear Greta,

Maybe you saw me on TV. If not, I hope you get cable. If you don't want cable, that's okay. I'm enclosing the article about me from last month's Oregonian. I'm the kid on the front page, stopping a train. I did it for the planet. And I did it for you. I even went to jail for it. Some things are worth doing time for, don't you agree?

Now that I've had all my rights restored, me and my friends are fighting to stop global warming. We tried to get the Supreme Court to help, but they refused because there's nothing in the Constitution to protect the planet.

So we're going to add an amendment that does.

Since the last time we went to Washington—to stop homework so kids in America could be more

72
★

like kids in Sweden—the Democrats won control of the House, but the Senate is split 50-50. Before we can even get the states to vote on an amendment, we have to convince 2/3 of the House and 2/3 of the Senate to pass it. You know how, in the Hunger Games, they say "may the odds be ever in your favor"? Well, with odds like ours, we'll probably get mowed down on the Capitol steps. But, hey, quitters never win and winners never quit, right?

Wish us luck.

Yours truly,

Alistair

P.S. Have you tried vegan cheese? I found a brand I like made from cashews. Melts pretty good.

P.P.S. If you don't want to use the mail system to write back, you can email me: ACWM@gmail.com. (It's my brand-new-this-year email. Stands for Alistair Climate Warrior Martin).

P.P.P.S. Regards to Roxy, Moses, and Beata.

"Do I sound gushy, Sam?"

"No."

"*I did it for you.* I should take that out, right?"

"*Did* you do it for her?"

"Well, she inspires me. And I really like her braids."

"Then leave it in. It's a good letter, Alistair. Send it."

• • •

A week goes by. Alistair points his home security camera at the mailbox so he can constantly monitor when the mail comes. He bakes vegan brownies for the mailman.

"Anything from overseas, Thomas?" he asks.

"Not today, Alistair."

Two weeks go by. I worry about my friend. He doesn't just flip through every magazine and catalog, searching for a letter from Sweden. He turns every page of every catalog and magazine.

"They use thin paper in Europe," he says. "Might stick to a page."

Three weeks go by. Alistair is now an expert on fleeces (L.L. Bean), native plants (*House & Garden*), how to fix a leaky faucet (*Family Handyman*), coral reefs (*National Geographic*), and anti-wrinkle creams (*Cosmopolitan*). All his practical knowledge can't fill the hole in his heart.

"I should have written her in Swedish," he says.

He downloads Duolingo on his phone.

• • •

We plan our trip to D.C. for spring break. The only two people standing between me and Congress are my parents.

"Dad, Mr. Kalman rebooked our suite at the Watergate Hotel. We're going to Congress to stop global warming."

"Okay, Sam. Good luck with that."

"Mom, we'll be gone—"

"Honey, it's not a good time for me to travel. And your dad is in the middle of a big remodel."

"I know. I'll be fine"—and then I say the words no mom wants to hear—"on my own."

My mother squints. Her arms pretzel across her chest. She sighs and says, "Follow me."

She walks to the Wall of Heights in the kitchen. It's literally where Sadie and I grew up.

"Back to the wall."

"Oh, please. Didn't we just do this a month—"

"Six months ago. On your birthday."

She opens a drawer, pulls out the pencil and the piece of cardboard she always uses to get a straight line.

"You're slouching."

I stand up straight, feel the cardboard come down on the top of my head, and see my mom's forehead in front of my face. Last time it was her chin in front of my face. When did I get taller than my mom?

"Two inches," she says.

No wonder my socks show. Maybe it's a good thing. Maybe

it's like those signs at an amusement park. MUST BE THIS TALL TO RIDE.

But it's not just about being tall enough, or old enough, to go. It's *needing* to.

"Mom, when you were my age, did you worry about the planet?"

"We worried about pollution."

"Yeah, but were you scared that there might not be a future? For your own kids? For everyone?"

"No, Sam. It never occurred to us."

"It does to me. It does to my friends. Every day, there's something scary in the news. Storms that drown people in their cars. Fires that burn up whole towns. Heat waves that old people can't survive. It's code red for humanity, Mom. We have to do something about it. *I* have to do something because, well . . ."

"Because we didn't."

We look at each other, and I nod. My mom sighs. It's one of those deep-breath sighs that says *You're right. I surrender.*

"Promise you'll call me each night?"

"How about text?"

"Call."

"Deal."

• • •

It doesn't go as well with Zoe and her grandma.

"She said I can't go," Zoe tells us.

"How come?"

"She'll worry about me so far from home."

"But we'll be with you. We'll keep you safe. Won't we, Mr. Kalman?"

"Yes, but if Betty doesn't give permission, we can't insist."

"Yeah, you can," I say. "With parents, you just gotta keep hounding them. Eventually they wear down and say yes."

"That's just it, Sam," Zoe says. "She's not my parents."

Mr. Kalman gives me a look and shakes his head, like he knows something about Zoe that I don't.

"My parents are dead," she says.

"Oh," I say. And I don't know what else to say, except I'm sorry. I'd like to know what happened, but it might be rude to ask.

"I was nine," she says. "They drove up the coast for their anniversary. Left me with Nana for the weekend. On the way back, there was an accident and, yeah. So if my nana is a little strict about me going out of town, I get it."

We're all quiet for a few seconds. Quiet and disappointed that Zoe can't come.

"Suppose we invite Betty along," Mr. Kalman says.

I'm surprised he'd even think of that. "You two aren't exactly friends, Mr. Kalman."

"I'm willing to endure her company if it means you get to come too, Zoe."

Just when he says this, Zoe's eyes go wide. She's looking over Mr. Kalman's shoulder at the hallway behind the lounge.

Where Betty just rolled up with her walker.

"With an invitation like that," she says, "how can a lady say no?"

She turns and rolls away.

Twenty minutes later I get a text from Zoe. *Good news. She's packing.*

• • •

On the plane, I'm in row 17, sitting between Zoe and Catalina. Jaesang and Alistair are behind us. Jaesang is reading a book on extreme weather. And Alistair is reading *Our House Is on Fire,* a memoir about Greta Thunberg and her family.

Across the aisle from me, Betty and Mr. Kalman are side by side but stone silent. I lean around Catalina and point to Betty's Ratify the ERA cap.

"I like your hat, Betty."

"Thank you, Sam. I'll get you one in D.C."

I try to catch Mr. Kalman's eye, and when I do, I give him a nod like, *Go on, talk to her.* He shrugs, glances at her cap, and says, "Were you there?"

"We were there," she says. "Mel and I never missed a march."

"Us too," Mr. Kalman says.

Things get quiet in row 17. Until Betty says, "Us?"

"Me and Miriam."

But he doesn't say more.

Then Alistair leans forward. "Guys, listen to this. Greta's mom is describing how Greta was bullied when she was young. Kids used to push her to the ground, get her to cry, make her hide in the bathroom. And when her mom told her everything would be okay, she'd make friends, Greta said, *I don't want to have a friend. Friends are children, and all children are mean.* Man, I'd like to give those kids a piece of my Swedish mind."

"Alistair," Jaesang says, "you're not Swedish."

"I know. But still."

He turns a page; he can't put the book down.

• • •

Sitting between two girls can be awkward, especially on a plane. So how'd I get stuck in the middle seat? By being a gentleman, I guess. Because when Zoe said she loves the window seat, and Catalina said she loves the aisle, I said, "I'm good with the middle," even though I'm really an aisle seat kind of guy.

I wonder if it's awkward for Mr. Kalman sitting next to Betty. I bet they'd have lots in common if they'd just start talking to each other. But he's working the crossword puzzle in his lap; she's reading a book on her Kindle. *All In* by Billie Jean King. I can see the title in supersize font.

Maybe Mr. Kalman will get stuck on a word and need Betty's help.

"Sam, *Animal Crossing* on the Switch?" Zoe says.

"Sure," I say.

We connect in Wi-Fi mode and start to play, and pretty soon it's not awkward anymore, and soon after that Zoe says, "This is my first time away from home since my parents' anniversary weekend."

I remember that she told us it happened when she was nine.

"So . . . three years ago?"

"Yeah. Last time we traveled, we flew to the Amazon. On a pilgrimage."

"Oh," I say. "Were your parents very religious?"

"Not that kind of pilgrimage. It was a quest to see a green basilisk lizard, a.k.a. *Basiliscus plumifrons*. My dad wanted to see one in the wild, 'cause in the wild, they do something you won't ever see them do in a cage."

"Reptiles give me the heebie-jeebies."

"They wouldn't, Sam, if you grew up with them like I did. We had a basement—my dad called it the nursery. It was all grow lights and terrariums, cockroaches and mealworms and frozen mice. And reptiles, of course. My dad raised them, and I got to name them. Have you ever held a panther chameleon?"

"Uh, no, can't say I have."

"They're softer than you'd think. Cool to the touch. Benny was my favorite. An ambilobe panther. We used to play peekaboo. His big eye always found me. Loved that little guy."

I ask her where Benny is now, and she tells me they had to give all the critters to Ed's Pet Shop in Glendale.

"They don't allow reptiles at the NoHo Senior Arts Colony," she says.

"No exceptions?"

"No exceptions."

Zoe looks out the window at the scattered clouds. I look at Zoe. Then I ask, "What do they do, the basilisk lizards? What is it you never get to see in a cage?"

"They walk on water. Their nickname is the Jesus lizard."

A funny name for a lizard, I think.

"So did you get to see one do it?"

"Sure did. Saw him run along the surface of a river too. He made it about fifteen feet."

Zoe gets lost in the memory.

"I guess your dad was pretty religious, after all," I say. "He found Jesus. And saw him walk on water."

We both laugh at that, then go back to *Animal Crossing*. We build a campsite together in the game.

10

The Man Who Knows
Everything

We fly to D.C. on Monday, and on Tuesday, Mr. Kalman takes us to the National Archives Building on Pennsylvania Avenue. If you saw the movie *National Treasure,* you know that this is where our founding documents are kept. The Declaration of Independence. The Constitution. The Bill of Rights.

He wants us to know just how huge—and how hard—our work ahead is going to be. So he introduces us to the man who knows everything.

"Guys, this is Mr. Becerra, our nation's archivist. He's in charge of all the official documents and records of the government. He also oversees the presidential libraries. If you have questions about America, the political process, or the Constitution, he's your go-to guy."

You'd expect a documents guy to be old and thin and wear thick glasses and maybe a bow tie around his neck. But Daniel

Becerra, the national archivist, looks more like your soccer coach or math teacher. Round face, no glasses, a friendly smile.

"I have a question," Alistair says to him. "How long does it take to amend the Constitution?"

"Are you patient?"

"Not really, Mr. Becerra. We're trying to save the planet."

"Then you can hope to beat the record for swiftest passage of an amendment, the Twenty-Sixth. From proposal to ratification, the total elapsed time was three months, eight days."

We look at each other, excited. With a timeline like that, we can make a difference now.

Catalina asks what the Twenty-Sixth Amendment was about. Mr. Becerra tells us it gave eighteen-year-olds the right to vote.

"Aren't you going to ask *why* it passed so swiftly?"

"Why did it?"

"To understand why, you need to know when."

"Okay, when did it pass?" Jaesang asks.

"July 1, 1971. What was happening in July of 1971?"

We look at each other and shake our heads.

"Vietnam," Betty says. "And young men age eighteen and over were being drafted. Many were dying, yet they didn't even have the right to vote."

Mr. Becerra nods at Betty. "The irony of that grim fact was

not lost on the lawmakers of a country whose founders had rebelled against the British for taxation without representation. And so, the Twenty-Sixth Amendment was passed in record time."

"Which one took the longest?"

"The Twenty-Seventh. It took two hundred and three years."

"*What?*" Alistair says. "The planet will be toast by then."

"How could something take so long to pass?" Jaesang asks.

"Well, the Bill of Rights originally had twelve amendments, not ten. The first provided for one representative for up to fifty thousand citizens. By that measure, we would now have six thousand members of Congress instead of four hundred and thirty-five. The second prohibited Congress from giving itself a pay raise. Any increase in pay couldn't take effect until after the next election. In 1789 those two were discarded. But in 1982, a college student at the University of Texas, Austin, had to do a research paper for his government class. He stumbled upon this unratified amendment about pay raises and noticed that there was no expiration date in the original text. He wondered, could it still be ratified all those years later? The thesis of his paper was, why not? Do you know what grade he received?"

"An A-plus," Mr. Kalman says.

"C. His professor thought it was a ridiculous idea. A *dead-letter issue,* she said. *It will never pass.* But C students are sometimes the smartest in the class."

Suddenly Alistair seems interested.

"Around this time, Congress was considering a hefty pay raise for itself, so the topic was much in the news. The C student, Gregory Watson, was working part-time for his state senator and told him about the dusty, forgotten amendment. The senator thought it was viable and brought the amendment to the Texas Legislature. Texas ratified it. So did New Jersey, Illinois, California, and thirty-four more states, including some that originally had voted against. On May 7, 1992, it was recorded by the national archivist as the Twenty-Seventh Amendment to the Constitution. And the University of Texas went back and changed Mr. Watson's grade to an A."

"Wow, that's a great story," Alistair says. "But—"

"If you like amendments, I'll tell you about some more."

"Maybe some other time, because we—"

"Who wants a glass of wine?" Mr. Becerra asks.

"I do," Betty says.

"I do," Alistair says. "For cooking purposes."

"You're too young. Only two of you have attained the legal drinking age. But in 1919, even Mr. Kalman and Ms. Betty would not be permitted a glass of wine. That's because the Eighteenth Amendment outlawed the production, sale, and consumption of spirits — alcoholic beverages."

"That bites," Alistair says.

"So thought many citizens of the time, though they would have expressed the sentiment by calling Congress a *killjoy*. In 1933, during the Great Depression, people were in serious need of a drink. Ten months later, the Twenty-First Amendment repealed the Eighteenth."

Alistair has been jiggling like a boy who's got something he has to let out.

"Nice. But the thing is — "

"Ladies, would you have voted for that?"

Zoe, Catalina, and Betty all nod.

"But only because the Nineteenth Amendment, proposed on June 4, 1919, and ratified on August 18, 1920, gave women the right to vote. Do you know how many votes it passed by?"

We all shake our heads no.

"Just one. Tennessee was the last state to vote. Their senate voted to ratify, but in the state house, there was a tie. Harry T. Burn, a twenty-four-year-old legislator, planned to vote against the amendment. But at the last minute he received a note from the one person who could change his mind."

"Eleanor Roosevelt!" Betty says.

"Nope."

"Amelia Earhart," Catalina guesses.

"Nope."

"The president," I say.

"His mother," Mr. Becerra says. "She told him she loved him and knew he'd do the right thing. So you see, the history of amendments is the history of our changing nation. Now, tell me about yours."

The first thing Alistair lets out is a huge sigh of relief. Now that he has Mr. Becerra's attention, he says, "Ours is going to protect the planet against climate change. We're going to guarantee everyone the right to a stable climate, clean air, and safe water."

Mr. Becerra is a man of many words, but right now he's speechless. I notice his eyebrows go up, come down, then go up again.

"You'll need a sponsor. Either your state assemblyperson or your representative in Congress. I suggest you find one in Congress. It is easier to get an amendment proposed there. Go to the House of Representatives—just down the street from here on Capitol Hill—and ask to see your representative. As soon as you get an appointment, tell them your plan. If you have further questions, on or off topic, come see me anytime Monday through

Friday from nine to five. Closed weekends and national holidays. And remember the wise words from the late great Jim Morrison. 'He who controls the media controls the mind.'"

"Wow," Alistair says on our way out. "That guy knows everything."

11

We Don't Have an Appointment

At nine the next morning, we walk up the Capitol steps and speak to a guard.

"Hi," I say. "We're here to see our representative."

"Which one? There are four hundred and thirty-five."

Jaesang asks Google who our representative is, and Google directs us to a search box on house.gov. We put in Alistair's zip code, and it gives us two possibilities, so we have to enter his address, and finally a name pops up.

"Marty Schiffrin," Jaesang says.

"Fourth floor Rayburn. 2438. Do you have an appointment?"

"No."

"That's the walk-up line."

He points to a line about two hundred people long.

Now it's two hundred and seven people long.

But it moves pretty fast. An hour later we're inside. Since it's ten o'clock, a lot of senators and representatives are just arriving. Mr. Kalman recognizes one of them: Representative Marty Schiffrin from California!

"Mr. Schiffrin, a moment of your time, please," Mr. Kalman says.

"You'll have to make an appointment on my website."

"But this boy is a constituent of yours."

"He doesn't look old enough to vote."

"I've been on television, sir. Perhaps you've seen *Master*—"

"You still need to make an appointment."

They step into an elevator. The doors start to close.

But Betty calls out— "Representative Schiffrin, we'd like to donate a million dollars to your reelection."

The doors open.

"Just kidding," she says. "But these children have a really important idea. You should hear them."

"They need an appointment."

This time the doors stay closed.

Jaesang whips out his phone, goes on Representative Schiffrin's website, and fills out the appointment form. It asks for a first, second, and third choice of dates.

Under all three he writes *NOW. THIS SECOND. CAN'T WAIT.*

A few minutes later he gets a response: *Your appointment with Representative Schiffrin's staff is scheduled for July 5.*

Three months away!

"That's how long it took to pass the Twenty-Sixth Amendment," Alistair says.

We figure that what goes up in an elevator must come down, so we camp out in the hallway by the same elevator. But you're not allowed to "camp out" in the halls of Congress, so we keep moving, literally pacing the halls for another two hours until—

A woman comes up to Alistair and says, "Weren't you on *MasterChef Junior?*"

"Yeah."

"You killed it with a Gruyère soufflé."

"You saw the finals?"

"I've been obsessed with cooking since I was a kid."

I notice Catalina's jaw drop and her mouth get wider and wider.

"Sam, do you know who that is?" she asks me.

"Yeah, some lady who saw Alistair on *MasterChef Junior.* She's a big fan of the show."

"It's AOC—Alexia Oracion-Cortina. She's the representative from Queens who came up with the Green New Deal."

And she just introduced herself to Alistair!

"Well, it's great to meet you, Alistair," she says. "What are you doing in D.C.?"

"Me and my friends came looking for a sponsor for our Planet Amendment."

"What Planet Amendment?"

"The one we wrote. To save the planet."

"I love it. Who's your representative?"

"Schiffrin. But his office won't see us 'til July."

"Do you have a draft? Do you know what you want it to say?"

Alistair turns to us. "Guys."

And we all recite, "A stable climate being necessary for the survival of life on Earth, the right of the planet to be free from pollution and unnatural warming shall not be infringed."

She looks at Alistair. "I'll sponsor your amendment. I'll introduce it on the House floor tomorrow."

"Really?"

"There's a quid pro quo, though. This is Congress, after all."

"Name your price, Ms. Oracion-Cortina."

"A handwritten copy of your Gruyère soufflé recipe. Signed by the chef."

Alistair smiles. "Deal."

They bump elbows on it.

• • •

The next day, we get a special pass to sit in on a session of Congress. The Speaker calls the House to order and asks the committee chairs to report on committee business. Then they take a break. Then they come back and take votes. Then they take a break. Then they come back and vote some more. Then they go to lunch. Then they come back, and the Speaker calls for additional house business. That's when AOC approaches the lectern.

"For what purpose does the representative from Queens rise?"

"Madam Speaker, I would like to introduce a resolution, H.R. 717, a proposed amendment to the Constitution."

The entire chamber goes silent.

"Under the jurisdiction of which committee?"

"The Select Committee on the Climate Crisis, Madame Speaker."

"Has it been drafted there?"

"No, Madam Speaker. The proposed amendment has already been drafted by . . . someone else."

"Who?"

"A legal team of children. They'd like to skip the usual drawn-out process of committee tinkering and put the amendment to the House for a vote. Immediately."

"Ms. Oracion-Cortina, this is highly irregular."

"As irregular as the matter is urgent, Madame Speaker."

The Speaker looks at her: Is she serious? AOC looks right back. She is.

"Without objection, we'll hear the amendment read out."

"Madame Speaker, I move that the authors of the amendment read it themselves."

"All right. The authors are recognized on the floor."

AOC nods at Alistair. He rises and says, "We call it the Planet Amendment." He turns to us, and together we chant, "A stable climate being necessary for the survival of life on Earth, the right of the planet to be free from pollution and unnatural warming shall not be infringed."

Dead silence in the chamber. The Speaker looks at us. She looks at Representative Cortina.

"Without objection, let's take a vote," she says.

"I object."

A representative from the other side of the chamber rises.

"The representative from Wyoming is recognized."

"Thank you, Madame Speaker. I object to the wording of the amendment. The planet is not a citizen of the United States. It can't have rights under the Constitution."

"I object to your objection," Alistair says. "The Twenty-First Amendment gave rights to beer, and it passed."

"No. It gave rights to the people to consume beer."

"Okay, so we'll change the wording. *The right of the people to*

95
★

inhabit a planet free from pollution and unnatural warming shall not be infringed. That better?"

"Representative from Wyoming? The language of the amendment has been revised."

"It's too disruptive, too radical. If you outlaw all human impacts on the climate, you'll outlaw some of the country's most profitable businesses."

"And save the planet!" comes a chorus from our row.

• • •

There are 435 members of Congress. In order for a proposed amendment to move on to the Senate, it needs to pass by a two-thirds majority.

In case you've never sat in on a congressional vote—and not a lot of people have—it happens fast and electronically. Each member of Congress has a voting machine in front of their seat, which would be a hacker's dream if you could get to it.

The clerk of the House reads out the tally. We get 289 votes for and 146 votes against.

"You realize what that means," Catalina says.

"We lost already?" Alistair says.

Math never was his thing.

"By two votes," Catalina explains. "We're moving on to the Senate."

12

The Senate Floor

Ever since he ran for president in 2016, Barney Saunders has been a hero of Mr. Kalman's. The two of them are what Mr. Kalman would call kindred spirits. Pretty far left in their politics. Old-school in how they talk. They even look alike, with thin gray hair and a lot of hand motions when they speak. And ever since Barney sat outside on a cold January morning wearing those now-famous mittens, he's been a hero of Catalina's too. "He didn't go on L.L. Bean.com and *buy* those mittens. He had a friend, a teacher, knit them for him."

Today we got to meet him. AOC walked us over, and Barney said he'd introduce our amendment right away.

He also called it "brilliant," which made Alistair blush.

"There's bound to be a debate," Mr. Kalman tells us. "I'd like Alistair to address the Senate."

"Me?"

"You're the one who stood in front of a train, Alistair. You have the vision—and the chutzpah—to sway a deeply divided Senate. But I warn you, the floor of the Senate can be a terrifying place. It looks much larger on TV than it is in real life. Behind you sit a hundred senators—fifty on the Republican side, fifty on the Democrat side. You can't imagine a more partisan split. It's your job to bring enough of them together—we need sixty-seven votes—to send the amendment on to the states for ratification."

There's a lot of partisan fighting over it, but the Democrats have put an end to the filibuster, which is this huge stalling technique that senators *used to* do when they wanted to delay a vote. They would basically stand up and talk for hours, rambling on and off topic until the other senators got so worn down, they gave up and went home. But without the filibuster, debate on our Planet Amendment moves along pretty fast.

The Senate minority leader, Butch McKinley, gives a long speech calling the amendment the work of radical climate terrorists. "It's an attempt to undermine the economic freedoms of this nation. I'll do everything in my power to stop it."

But the junior senator from Georgia, a preacher-turned-politician named Ralph Walker, says, "And I'll do everything in my power to pass it. We are living through climate events of biblical proportions." (He should know.) "This amendment, I believe, is humanity's last hope."

But for every senator on our side, it seems there's another one against us. This time it's Tim Crews, from Texas, who rises.

"The senator from Texas is recognized."

"I rise, Mr. Majority Leader, to question the sanity of this proposed amendment."

Alistair jumps to his feet. "And I rise to defend it!"

"How can we be one hundred percent certain that climate change is real?"

"It's like the good senator from Texas himself said. *I'll believe in climate change when Texas freezes over.* Well, Texas froze over. They even had a snownado. But you were in Cancún at the time, so you might've missed it."

"Okay, it's real, I'll accept that. But how do you know we caused it? There have been ice ages long before humans were around."

"It's something called science, Senator. Can we show you a few slides?"

Majority Leader Schneider nods. Jaesang flicks on his mini projector and aims it at the wall. It shows the CO_2 levels from 1950 to today. It looks like a graph of Tesla stock over the last five years . . . rising at a forty-five-degree angle.

"That's how much carbon dioxide we've added to the Earth's atmosphere. We doubled it in fifty years. Before the Industrial Revolution, CO_2 levels hovered between 175 and 275 parts per million. Now it's nearing 600. If we keep on burning fossil fuels, by 2050 we could double it again. Next slide, please."

It shows a second graph: *Global Temperature Rise, 1950–2050*. It's practically the same line.

"If we don't flatten the curve by 2050, the planet will be on average two degrees Celsius hotter. Take a look at what we've done to the Arctic."

Jaesang projects a series of images of the Arctic Circle over the last twenty years. You can literally see the shrinking of the polar ice caps.

"Zoe, will you explain this to them?"

Zoe jumps up. "As the planet warms," she says, "the permafrost melts. Ice turns to shallow lakes. Bacteria break down plants and animals, but they don't break them down all the way. Imagine half-rotting roadkill without enough bacteria to finish the job. Instead of turning into water and carbon dioxide, the plants and animals turn to methane. And methane warms the atmosphere at eight times the rate of CO_2."

"So the planet gets hotter," Senator Crews says. "We have air-conditioning, don't we?"

"How old are your kids, Senator?" Jaesang says.

"Ten and twelve."

Jaesang flashes another slide: Earth in 2050.

"When your youngest is as old as you are now, this is

what her world will look like. More Category Five hurricanes, one hundred and sixty billion dollars' worth of coastal property underwater. Devastating floods like we saw in Germany, Belgium, and New Jersey. More than fifty days of over ninety-degree weather. Plus the record freeze *some* of us saw in Texas and Louisiana."

He shows a series of pictures from the wildfires, orange skies and ash, heaps of molten metal that used to be cars, chimneys where whole houses stood.

"Eleven million acres burned in the last three summers alone. In the future, it will cost twelve billion dollars more in energy costs to keep humans comfortable."

Now Catalina jumps up. "And what about all the people who don't have access to air-conditioning, clean water, or food? Where will they go? You'll see a mass migration ten times the size of the Ukranian refugee crisis."

Jaesang jumps up too. "Last year, the people who name the hurricanes ran out of English names. There were more than twenty-six severe storms, so they had to start the alphabet over again with Greek letters.

It's my turn to jump up. "And there's something else. Storms are like teenagers. They absorb a ton of stress that builds up over time. Eventually they rage. But as ocean temperatures rise, the teenager acts more like a two-year-old. She goes from anger to

101
★

full-on tantrum in record speed. Climatologists call this rapid intensification. Last year ten storms had it."

Now all five of us kids are standing. Standing on the Senate floor. Which happens to be stone silent.

"Senator Crews?"

The senator from Texas is flummoxed. I love that word.

"And let's not forget the animals who share our planet," Zoe says.

She glances at Jaesang, who projects the species chart. It shows the decline in total animal species. The exact opposite of the CO_2 curve.

"Since we've had this one debate in just this one hour, six more species have vanished from the Earth. That's one hundred and fifty a day, more than four thousand a month, fifty thousand a year. It's not just that these animals are cute. It's that they're crucial to the diversity of nature. We need that diversity for our own survival. If we don't stop climate change, humans could be on this list by 2150."

Now Alistair leans into the mic. "Senators on both sides, if the smoke alarms in here went off right now, you'd all jump up and save yourselves, right? I mean, those things are *loud*. Well, the planet's smoke alarms have been screaming at us for years. Droughts. Floods. Heat domes. Disappearing ice. Why can't you hear the siren? I know people are scared of change. We've only known how to power up this great economy by burning fossil fuels. But the Planet Amendment will force us to see a new way ahead. It'll get us up and out of this burning house before it's too late."

A *lot* of senators rise to their feet and applaud. More than half, I'd say, by the sound.

A senator from Colorado says she wants to add something to the amendment.

"Mr. Majority Leader, I believe the amendment has merit. But it's too abrupt. It needs a start date—five years from ratification—and a time limit of three months."

Five years from ratification . . . I guess that makes sense. You have to give industries time to retool their factories and make them green. Also to retrain their workers for a new green economy.

"One year," Alistair says.

"Four years," the senator says.

"Two."

"Four."

"One."

"But you just said two."

"You didn't budge."

"Okay, three."

"Deal."

Man, Alistair would make a good negotiator.

But the time limit for ratification . . .

"Three months?" Alistair says. "That would make it the second-fastest amendment ever to pass."

"If the matter it as urgent as you claim, three months is enough time."

The majority leader looks at us. Alistair hesitates.

"How about nine months?

"Three."

"At least give us five. 'Til the end of the summer."

"Deal."

Alistair whips out his recipe book and scrawls. Then he gets stuck and turns to Catalina for help. She takes his pencil from him and starts to write. When she's done, she hands it back to Alistair, who reads aloud to the chamber.

"'This article shall not take effect unless it shall have been ratified as an amendment to the Constitution by the legislatures of three-fourths of the several states, within five months from the date of the submission hereof to the states by Congress. If ratified, this amendment shall become the law of the land exactly three years from the date of ratification.'

"That better?"

• • •

Unlike the House, the Senate votes in person. Senators come forward by roll call and vote aye or nay—or, in the case of John

McCain, who cast the tie-breaking vote that saved the Affordable Care Act a few years ago, thumbs up or thumbs down. The senators vote in alphabetical order by state.

After about forty-five minutes of ayes and nays, we're at 58 votes in favor of sending the amendment to the states and 32 votes against.

With ten states left, we need eight more votes.

Both of Vermont's senators vote aye. Thanks, Barney.

Same with Virginia. We only need four more yeses.

We get two more from Washington.

The next state is West Virginia. It has one Democrat and one Republican.

Both vote nay.

Wisconsin has one Democrat and one Republican.

Both vote nay.

It's not looking good. We still need two more senators to vote yes.

The last two states are Wisconsin and Wyoming.

We get one yes from Wisconsin.

Wyoming is a big problem. It's a cattle rancher's state. A coal state. Why would its senators vote yes to shut down ranching and coal?

The first senator votes nay.

But Wyoming also has Grand Teton National Park. Old

Faithful. And the Grand Prismatic Spring. The state gets tons of money from tourism . . . and a giant wind farm.

The second one votes aye.

Catalina knows what that means. So do I . . . and Jaesang and Mr. Kalman and Betty and Zoe. We're all smiling, looking at Alistair, who may be a genius in the kitchen, but he's a goofball at math.

"Why are you guys so happy? How many more votes do we need?"

"Zero," Catalina says. "We just got the sixty-seventh senator to vote yes."

"You mean our amendment got through?"

The clerk of the Senate makes it official. "By a vote of sixty-seven to thirty-three, the proposed Planet Amendment moves on to the state legislatures. They have one hundred and fifty days to ratify, or it is null and void."

"Now what?" we ask Mr. Kalman.

"Like Jim Morrison said, now we control the message."

13

Living the Truth

We decide to shoot a video to get kids across the country to bug their parents to bug their state representatives to ratify the amendment. Our campaign is called Planet Power.

Alistair has a huge oak tree in his backyard. It's sixty feet tall, with a dripline thirty feet around. Alistair says his oak tree is more than 350 years old, so we think it's the perfect place to start our video.

"Oak tree, oak tree, what do you see?" Alistair says, tweaking the words to his favorite children's book.

Jaesang answers, *"I see a bird's nest falling from me."*

Next, we shoot a close-up of James, Alistair's pet tortoise.

"James Beard, James Beard, what do you see?"

We get Mr. Kalman to voice James.

"I see ashes falling on me."

We don't have a pet polar bear, but Catalina's little sister has a stuffed one. Her little sister is pretty grown up, though, because she tells us a stuffed polar bear will look fake, and if we really want to convince people, we should use a real one.

We copy some footage from the Nat Geo channel, of a desperate polar bear trying to find an iceberg to rest on.

"White Bear, White Bear, what do you see?"

And Zoe says, *"I see my future shrinking from me."*

We take another piece of footage from a different documentary. This one is about the rainforest, and it shows a frightened baby chimpanzee. Behind him, we hear a chain saw growl and see a giant tree fall.

"Little Chimp, Little Chimp, what do you see?"

"I see my mommy taken from me."

For our last shot we all climb to different branches of Alistair's oak. His mom voices the last question.

"Children, children, what do you see?"

"We see a crisis. Don't you agree?"

Then, one by one, we swing off the branches and land together at the base of the tree.

"The Planet Amendment needs your vote. Say yes. While there's still time."

That night I add music, and Jaesang clicks upload.

• • •

In a little ceremony in the lounge at the NoHo Senior Arts Colony, Alistair asks us all to take the Planet Pledge:

I pledge allegiance
To the Planet
And all the life upon it.
I promise to —
Refuse what I don't need
Reuse what I already have
Repair what I can
Recycle what I can't

So, for instance, I refuse to take long showers. Alistair said to pick a song under three minutes and play it while you shower; when the song ends, the shower ends.

I chose "In Summer" from *Frozen*. It's under two minutes.

My dad chose "Stairway to Heaven," the 1973 live version. It's ten minutes and fifty-three seconds long.

But first he runs the water for two minutes to get it hot.

"Dad, you can't take a thirteen-minute shower. It's terrible for the planet."

"Sadie is away at college. You take showers under two minutes. Mom's in and out in under three. So I've got a hot water budget I can spend."

With offsets like those, my dad has a carbon footprint the size of Texas.

"Dad, shut the fridge," I told him last week.

"I'm trying to decide what to eat."

"Decide before you open."

"How's that make sense, Sam? I can't see through the door."

The next time he opened the fridge, he got his hand smashed when the door swung back.

I had installed an FS-1306 Grade 3 Spring Hydraulic Door Closer. Probably set the tension a bit too high.

Yesterday I caught him throwing away an electric toothbrush.

"You know that has heavy metals, right? They'll be in the landfill for five hundred years."

"But the battery won't hold its charge."

"So replace the battery and recycle the old one."

He shrugged and said he'd already clicked Buy Now on Amazon.

In the weeks that follow, we all start "living the truth," as Jaesang calls it. He's been practicing Buddhism and, he tells us, everything is interconnected. Even small acts of conservation make a difference, because if you multiply them by enough people, you get real change.

But I have to change my shower song. "In Summer," I found out, is too short.

"Sam," my mom said the other night, "are you showering every day?"

"Every morning. Why?"

"Using soap?"

"Of course."

"Scented?"

"I think so."

"Maybe take a little more time."

That's all she had to say for me to get it. I'm not just getting taller. I'm getting stinkier too.

I switched my song to "Sunshine of My Life" by Stevie Wonder. And I switched my soap to Dove Minerals + Sage for men. And the next time my mom got close enough to sniff, she said, "Ahhh. My sweet-smelling son."

I offset the longer showers by giving up meat.

My mom is living the truth too. Every time she sells a house, she asks the buyers and sellers to each throw in $5,000 to make the house greener. Her *New Owner, New World* plan has already replaced seven gas furnaces with electric heat pumps and hot water heaters. She even got one owner to kick in $15,000 toward solar panels.

My dad needs help living the truth. I become a climate warrior at war with his own dad.

First, I unplug the clothes dryer.

"Dad," I say, "the dryer stopped working."

"Check the circuit breaker, Sam."

"Already did. I think it's broken."

"We can't afford a new one right now."

"I know. That's why I rigged a rope."

I take him outside and show him the fifty-foot clothesline I put up. It stretches from one side of the backyard to the other. I strung it toward the part of the yard where, in the shade, there's always a breeze.

Our whole family's laundry, hanging by clothespins, swings in the wind. It looks like a dance party without hands and feet.

"Think that'll work?" Dad says.

"'Course it will. And our clothes will smell sweet as spring."

We just cut our carbon footprint by twenty percent.

Catalina decides to give up shopping.

"I don't shop anymore," she says. "I swap."

She tells me about this website, Depop, where you can trade your old clothes for someone else's. It's a way to update your wardrobe without things going to waste.

"Zoe told me about it."

"It's not just for girls, Sam," Zoe says. "Guys swap too."

"But I mostly wear track pants and T-shirts."

"Yeah, but when you outgrow them—and you have been growing a lot this year—instead of tossing them and buying new ones, you can swap with someone else. And the best part—you'll be disrupting the fashion industry that cares more about profit than the ethical treatment of its workers."

"And," Catalina says, "you'll cut down on the pollution that comes from companies that spill their dyes into rivers."

Cat starts a Swap Don't Shop campaign at school. She sets up a Stop 'n' Swap table by the cafeteria. Kids donate the clothes they've outgrown or gotten tired of, and they get to pick something new. It becomes an obsession among all grades because everyone likes to see how other people look in their clothes. It also gets confusing. Like yesterday we were playing 5 on 5 full court, and right before the bell rang, I passed the ball to Jaesang, but it wasn't Jaesang. It was Kevin in eighth grade, who'd swapped his Cavaliers jersey for Jaesang's Bucks one! Kevin scored on the turnover. A loss for my team, but a win for the planet.

Our houses are living the truth, too. The thermostats are all set to 65 degrees for heat and 77 for cool. They're controlled by Alistair, who found out you can get free smart thermostats from the power company and installed them in all our homes. He monitors them from an app on his phone. He's trying to prove a point, that humans are more adaptable than we think and can get by with less energy.

Problem is, when you give a twelve-year-old boy the controls to your heat and lights, who's going to control *him*? The other night my dad got home late from work and made himself a salami sandwich. (I had secretly replaced the real salami in the package with tofulami, so I was watching him carefully to see if he'd taste the difference.)

He was about to take a bite when—poof—the lights went out.

"Power failure?" he said.

"Power savior," I said.

It was nine o'clock, when Alistair had programmed our lights to automatically go off.

On his way to bed, Dad tried to raise the thermostat to 68.

Alistair brought it back down to 65.

They got into a thermostat war, but I told my dad there was no way he could win. "As soon as you fall asleep, Alistair will turn off the heat."

I tossed him a wool beanie for the night.

• • •

Dear Greta,

Hej! Läget.

If someday you move to the United States and marry an American citizen,* you could have dual citizenship. But—and there's always a but—you wouldn't be able to run for president. That's because the so-called Arnold Amendment didn't get ratified. It's called the Arnold Amendment for Arnold Shw—hang on a sec, I gotta Google how to spell his name—Schwarzenegger. He wanted to be president. But the Constitution says you have to be "at least 35 years old and a native-born U.S. citizen." Arnold was born in Austria. Hence the accent the people of California loved so much, and the people of the world loved so much, especially in Terminator when he said, "I'LL BE BACK." He was so popular that his friends in D.C. thought he could be president. In 1993 Congress passed an amendment that would have given any "native-born or naturalized" citizen eligibility to run. The amendment only got eight out of fifty states to ratify. So even though Arnold said, "I'LL BE BACK," he wasn't.

I hope our Planet Amendment does better. So far we've gotten six states to ratify: California, Oregon, Washington, New York, Massachusetts, and Vermont.

Vises!

Alistair

*I'm sure you'll have loads of offers. Just be sure you choose someone who can cook.

• • •

By late April, ten states have ratified the Planet Amendment. Three voted no. We need twenty-eight more yeses out of the thirty-seven that haven't voted yet.

In May, when Sadie comes home for her summer break, she makes an announcement: "I've decided not to get pregnant."

"At nineteen," Mom says, "a good decision."

"At any age. I'm not going to have kids."

She says she's been inspired by our Planet Power campaign. She did some research on population growth, and it's pretty scary. Right now, global population is on its way to eight billion people. Scientists think the planet can support up to nine billion. The thing is, each human, over their lifetime, adds about ten thousand metric tons of CO_2 to the atmosphere. By not having children, Sadie says, she can help slow global warming.

It's hard to go against the science, but I was hoping to be an uncle someday.

"I was hoping to be an uncle someday," I say.

"You can be, Sam. I might adopt."

That's good. Still, there are things about my big sister that I'd like to see reproduced in a little kid. Like the fierce way she sticks up for me, or the brave way she talks to authority figures, or the brilliant way she argues a case.

And there are things about Sadie's mom, who died when

Sadie was five, that I'll bet Sadie would like to see again in a kid of her own. But I don't mention that. If she wants to slow the population growth by one child, it's up to her.

"What if the kid you were going to have but decided not to would have grown up to invent a new energy source that would save the planet and all humanity from extinction?"

I can't help it. It's my last, best argument for why she should have a kid.

"Sam," she says, "what makes you think that child isn't already born?"

She just blew up my argument. Not only that. It gives me hope.

14

Action

"Everybody pick a state," Mr. Kalman says. We're crammed into his 643-square-foot one-bedroom apartment at the NoHo Senior Arts Colony. The board voted to kick us out of the lounge because we made too much noise, consumed too many snacks, and turned the pool table into our personal work space. Three violations of the community rules.

So things are cozy. Instead of a pool table, we've spread out our notes on Mr. Kalman's coffee table. Instead of a big kitchen, we keep our snacks in a small one. And instead of bothering the whole community, we'll just be annoying Betty upstairs.

Jaesang reports that our Planet Power video has gotten 250,000 likes on TikTok and another 175,000 on Instagram. We're off to a good start.

But we'll need a miracle to get thirty-eight state legislatures to ratify.

Mr. Kalman unrolls a huge map of the United States. He's

colored the states we've won so far in green, the states we've lost in red, and the ones that haven't voted in white. Our map looks like this:

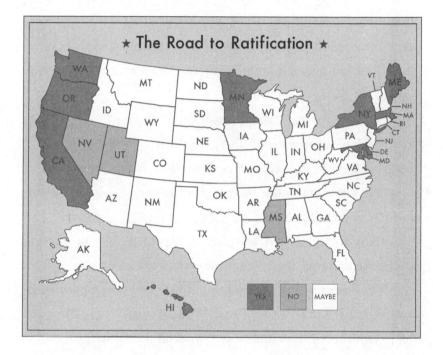

★ The Road to Ratification ★

Alistair and Catalina are going to work the Big Sky states: Montana and Wyoming.

Zoe and Jaesang will take on Texas and West Virginia.

And Mr. Kalman and I set our sights on one of the hardest states to win: Louisiana.

In Texas and Louisiana, there are as many oil and gas pipelines as there are people.

In Wyoming there's meat on every menu.

In West Virginia there's coal in most of the power plants. A miner in many families.

"We need to take disruptive action," Alistair says.

"I say we find out where the governors' kids go to school and kidnap them," Catalina says.

"No kidnapping," Mr. Kalman says.

"Let's blow up their oil and gas refineries," Alistair says.

"No blowing up oil and gas refineries," Mr. Kalman says.

"We could blockade their ports," Jaesang suggests. "Pour seawater in their pipelines."

"No blockades. No seawater in pipelines. If you disrupt commerce in Texas, there's no necessity defense."

"We'll march, then," Zoe says. "That's what my nana always says. March."

"On wheels," Catalina adds. "We'll hit the capitals of all the states that haven't signed."

• • •

As soon as school's out, we invite every kid in America to march. From sea to shining sea, up and down the Keystone XL pipeline, through the clear-cut forests of Montana, under the gray-black skies of Tennessee and West Virginia, and across the heartland of many cows, kids across America march—or roll—for our cause. And if there's one things kids have a lot of, it's wheels. Skateboard wheels, bicycle wheels, tricycle wheels; wheels on scooters, wheels on Heelies; wheels on Radio Flyers; wheels on a Segway for Mr. Kalman; wheels on an e-trike for Betty. Or, in Alistair's case, just one wheel, on his electric monocycle. All across the country, kids post videos of more than a hundred marches. They get ten thousand shares, more than a million likes. We just spawned a new army of climate warriors.

I know we're supposed to swap, not shop, but Zoe designed Planet Power T-shirts for all of us to wear. On the front is a picture of the planet, with climate facts as pop-outs: Portland 114°, Death Valley 130°, Dallas 6°. Acres burned across western states: 2019, 1 million; 2020, 2 million. Rainfall records: Tennessee, 22 inches in 24 hours. Predicted species loss to climate change by 2050: 50 percent.

On the back of the shirt is the text of the Planet Amendment in small print and, in large, the word RATIFY.

We order a thousand shirts and post them for sale on our Planet Power website.

A week later we have orders for ten thousand more.

Our video is up to thirty million likes on TikTok. Our Go-FundMe raises eleven million dollars. We use it to buy ad time on TV and on billboards along the same highways where oil tankers race back and forth between refineries and gas stations. In Galveston, Texas, you can't drive along Highway 45 without seeing Zoe's banner of Mother Earth choking under a smoky sky with the caption RATIFY. And another one in downtown Dallas, with a photo of that very street frozen in snow: REMEMBER THE BIG FREEZE. CLIMATE CHANGE IS REAL.

Mother Earth is on signs held up to the white marble capitols in Baton Rouge, Boise, Helena, and Houston. She's the good-morning warning to every state senator and assembly member on their way to work in Madison, Pierre, Lincoln, and Charleston. Thanks to our guerrilla ad tactics, stop signs all across America now say things like STOP THE ISLAND OF PLASTIC; STOP THE DYING CORAL REEFS; STOP THE ICE MELT; STOP KILLING TREES.

• • •

We track down the most influential people in any state: the governors' grandchildren. The youngest is Jimmy, a five-year-old boy in Montana whose summer cooking class is thrilled to be having a visit from last year's *MasterChef Junior* winner. Alistair is their guest of honor and gives them a cooking lesson.

"Today, boys and girls, you're going to learn how to make Wilbur in a Blanket. It's a recipe I made up inspired by one of my favorite books."

"Wilbur, like in *Charlotte's Web*?" a girl in pigtails asks.

She's wearing our Planet Power T-shirt in extra small.

"Yes."

"I don't want to eat Wilbur," another kid says, and—this is great—he starts to cry. Turns out *he's* Jimmy, the governor's grandson.

"Well . . . Jimmy," Alistair says, "that's the nice thing about my Wilbur in a Blanket recipe. Just like Charlotte, I found a way to save Wilbur's life."

"She writes 'some pig' in her web."

"I use mushrooms."

For some reason, the word makes a bunch of five-year-olds laugh.

"No, really. I use mushrooms instead of piggies. And by the time people figure out there's no pork in these, Wilbur has made a big getaway from the farm. So let's learn how to prepare Wilbur in a Blanket, and let's give them as a special treat to, I don't know, how about our grandparents? And *after* they've tasted and said *yum,* you can spill the secret. Tell them that Wilbur got away. And tell them that the planet would be healthier if we didn't raise so many animals for food. And while you have your grandparents' attention—"

He's looking right into little Jimmy's eyes, I swear—

"Tell them that you love them. But that you'd love them even more if they supported the Planet Amendment."

123
★

If all else fails, Alistair would make a great brainwasher of little kids.

In Wyoming, Catalina finds out that Evan, the governor's sixteen-year-old grandson, gives horseback riding lessons at Singletree Stables outside of Cheyenne. Catalina signs up. Her plan is to ride alongside him and strike up a conversation about the planet. But when it comes time to matching people with horses, she freezes.

"Have you ridden a horse before?" the instructor asks. He looks like he's around sixteen, but she hasn't seen a picture of the governor's grandson, so she can't be sure it's him.

If she says yes, he might put her up front on a fast horse.

If she says no, he might give her a poky horse in the rear.

"Do I look like I've been on a horse before?" she asks.

"I got a hunch that says yeah."

"Where do *you* ride during the lesson?"

"Up front, so I can lead the way. But if you need a little extra help, Evan over there always rides in back."

She glances over at a tall, thin teenage boy in skinny jeans, roughed-up boots, and a cowboy hat behind his head, hanging on a cord.

"Just kidding," Catalina says. "This is my first time."

The instructor calls out, "Newbie, Evan."

Evan nods toward Catalina. She's got him just where she wants him.

We send Betty to Pennsylvania, where she joins a knitting club hosted by the governor's daughter and her two teenage girls. She followed their Instagram and messaged them that she'd be visiting the Keystone State and could she come to a knitting session.

A few days later, the governor of Pennsylvania announces his support for the Planet Amendment. Meanwhile, Mr. Kalman and I head south to Louisiana, where the governor is too young to have any grandkids. But his teenage son, Jessie, has a zydeco band at the local high school — and they're playing a dance this weekend. But his piano player got hired at the last minute to play oldies at a seventy-fifth anniversary party at the Baton Rouge Country Club.

Of course, there's no such party at the Baton Rouge Country Club. When the piano player shows up, he'll be pretty surprised. At least he got paid in advance by Mr. Kalman, who Venmoed him the money.

And wouldn't you know, the morning of the dance, there's a street busker come all the way from Los Angeles, a twelve-year-old boy, playing *Zydeco Stomp* music outside the governor's mansion.

On his way to school, Jessie Miller stops to talk to the piano-playing boy who, I have to say, plays a sick beat on his portable keyboard.

"Hey, I like your music," he says.

"Thanks," I say.

"How old are you?"

"Twelve. You?"

"Sixteen. Listen, I've got a gig tonight. I need someone on keys. Feel like earning a hundred bucks?"

"Sure," I say.

The gig goes great—we're a super popular band—and afterward, on our way out of the school gym, we see this old guy holding a sign: SAVE THE PLANET: RATIFY.

Jessie turns to walk away from the old guy with the sign —Mr. Kalman.

"Aren't you sick of all this climate talk?" he says to me.

"Yeah," I say, trying to play it cool. "Seems like it's always in the news."

We walk on a bit. "Of course, it is a big problem," I add. "And maybe that amendment will help."

"I'm against it," Jessie says. "Hundred percent."

"Aren't you worried about the future?"

"That's why I'm against the amendment," he says. "It'll bankrupt our state."

He tells me that the biggest industries in Louisiana are chemicals, oil and gas, and cows.

"What about fishing? There's a lot of shrimp in the gulf. Don't you want those waters to be clean?"

"We can't survive on shrimp alone."

"What about storm surge? Aren't you worried about more Katrinas? More Idas?"

"If the government tells us we can't make chemicals anymore, can't drill for oil and gas or raise cattle, then people won't have jobs. In the short term, more folks will die from starvation than from floods."

"What the about the long term?" I ask.

Jessie shrugs. At the end of the path there's a limo waiting for him. He says good night to me, gives me his cell number, and says I should text if I'm ever in town again. "I can always use a good keyboarder," he says and walks away.

Sadie would've been more convincing.

In West Virginia, the governor's granddaughter is a seventh-grader named Melina. Her hobby is training AKC champion dogs. We sent Jaesang there with his grandpa to infiltrate a dog show.

"I don't know anything about purebred dogs," Jaesang had said.

"Well, Catalina is riding horses in Wyoming," I said. "Betty is in Pennsylvania learning how to knit. I'm playing zydeco in Louisiana. Alistair is cooking with little kids in Montana. And Zoe is making signs to put up across the country. So that leaves you."

"What am I supposed to do, pose as a cocker spaniel?"

"Bulldog's more your breed."

I hope he had better luck than I did in Louisiana.

• • •

After our early summer march, with strategic persuasion of governors' grandkids, our map looks like this:

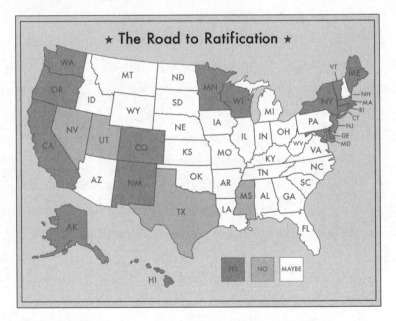

Eighteen states have ratified. We need twenty more.

Nebraska is a holdout. Their biggest industry is cattle farming. If our amendment gets ratified, thousands of people will lose their jobs. One of them comes up to us on the steps of the capitol in Omaha. Two kids hold her hands.

"I appreciate what you're doing for the planet," she says. "But I work in a meat processing plant. I don't know what else I'd do to support my children."

What do I say to her? Do I say, *If we don't change our ways, your children will struggle to survive?* Do I say, *Even the cattle that graze the fields here in Nebraska—they'll struggle to survive?*

"We need a head start," I say, "to make the planet healthy enough to support your kids."

"How will I feed them if I lose my job?"

Her question scares me.

Then I remember something Alistair told me on the train the other day. In the future, he said, we won't need to raise cattle to eat meat. We'll just sequence the DNA and print it in a lab. It's happening now in Sweden.

"Ma'am," I say, "in the future we'll just print meat from our refrigerators. Eventually there won't be any more need to kill cows."

"No," she says. "Just say no."

She raises her voice and says it again. It gets echoed by another mom. Their two voices turn into four, then twenty, then a chant that drowns ours out.

Here in Nebraska, Just Say No is louder than Just Say Yes. It's louder in Idaho too. Louder in Kentucky.

But in Pennsylvania, the legislators say yes. And they say yes in New Hampshire and Virginia. Yes in Georgia.

No in Alabama. No in South Dakota.

But yes in the Carolinas. Yes in Illinois.

• • •

Later in the summer, we regroup at Mr. Kalman's apartment and study the map. We have twenty-seven yeses and eleven nos. Twelve states haven't voted yet. We need eleven more for the amendment to pass.

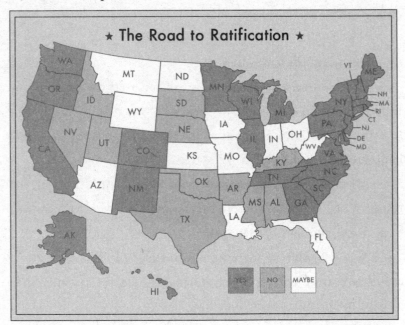

★ The Road to Ratification ★

"I'm afraid it's not looking good, kids," Mr. Kalman says. "The polls are against us in the remaining states. In Wyoming, the cattle industry is outspending us two to one. In Louisiana it's three to one — the oil and gas industry is lobbying the legislature hard."

"Maybe the people in Louisiana are getting sick of record-breaking rain," Jaesang says.

"What about West Virginia?"

Mr. Kalman shakes his head. "You know how their governor made his billions?"

"Please don't say coal."

"Coal."

"What about Iowa?" Alistair says. "They grow tons of food there. If we could show them what climate change will do to their crops . . ."

"I still have hope for Wyoming," Catalina says.

"We need to take symbolic action," I say. "Something the whole world can witness."

It's quiet in Mr. Kalman's apartment . . . until his doorbell rings.

"Sam?"

I get up, go to the door, and open it.

Betty and Zoe are standing on the other side. Zoe holds

a basket bursting with color—deep purple, red, dark orange—and brimming with large round shapes.

"Heirlooms?" Alistair says, appearing beside me at the door. His eyes are practically slicing the tomatoes.

"We grew them from seeds," Betty says. "And we brought some as a peace offering. An apology for the water that dripped onto your balcony . . . a hundred and eighty days ago."

Mr. Kalman comes to the door. He leans toward the basket and sniffs. "Alistair," he says, "there's some romaine in the fridge. A ripe avocado on the counter. And Thousand Island dressing in a glass bowl." He turns to Betty and Zoe. "Join us for lunch?"

It doesn't take Alistair long to make individual plates of romaine, sliced avocado, and heirloom tomatoes with a swirl of Thousand Island on top.

"Now *that* is how a tomato is supposed to taste," Mr. Kalman says, the corner of his mouth dripping juice.

"You grew these from seeds, really?" Jaesang says.

"Right upstairs on her balcony," Zoe says with pride.

I think back to the first day I came over. The seed pack said seventy-five days until first fruit. The plants have been growing for 105 more days. Seeds in February, plump sweet tomatoes in August. It's magic.

Then Zoe tells us there are ten thousand cultivars, or variet-

ies, of tomato plants. She names a few. Beefsteak. Campari. Early
Girl. Jersey Boy. Jubilee. Kumato. San Marzano. Montserrat.

"These are Cherokee Purple, Ferris Wheel, and Rosella
Purple."

"Imagine all those tomatoes on one plate," Jaesang says.

"Their *seeds* are all in one place, you know," Zoe says. "All
ten thousand and more."

"No way. There's nowhere big enough."

"Seeds are tiny, guys. There's a place that can hold up to two
and a half billion seeds. Right now it has five hundred million.
Seeds from all the edible plants on Earth—and different kinds
of those plants. It keeps them safe from a natural disaster, climate change, or a nuclear war. Almost every country keeps boxes
of seeds there, as backups, in case the world's food supply is ever
threatened. They call it the Doomsday Vault because if that day
ever comes, we'll all need seeds to survive."

"Where is this Doomsday Vault?"

"In Svalbard. On an island halfway between Norway and
the North Pole."

I start to think ... Could climate change threaten the
world's food supply? Droughts might cause crops to fail. Higher
temperatures might burn plants. Erosion might wreck the soil.
If that happens, those seeds could be humanity's most valuable
resource.

"How many countries have put seeds in the vault?" I ask.

"Two hundred and twenty-three. Even North Korea has a few boxes."

Mr. Kalman said no kidnapping, but I'm pretty sure he meant no kidnapping kids. Seeds, on the other hand . . .

"Who guards it?"

"The Norwegian Home Guard. But it's isolated, Sam. It would take a real adventurer, with really warm clothes, to travel all the way to Svalbard just to visit seeds."

"I don't want to just visit the seeds," I say. "I want to occupy the seed bank."

He looks at me. They're all looking at me now.

"Think of the publicity. Two hundred twenty-three countries. I'll bet a few of them are trading partners with the states we need. Iowa for sure. Probably Wyoming too, with all the beef it raises."

I look right at Mr. Kalman. He looks right at me. We've been through a lot together, my old neighbor and me. We know each other well enough to know that when our eyes lock like this, something big is about to happen.

"It's a wild idea, Sam."

"I know."

"Risky too. We could get hurt."

"I know."

"But we'd get a lot of attention."

"From the whole world."

"Might get arrested too."

"Wouldn't be the first time," Alistair says.

Mr. Kalman thinks. He thinks and he nods.

"Kids," he says, "who wants to take a field trip?"

"Where to, Mr. Kalman?" Jaesang asks.

"Norway."

I smile. And Alistair says, "Norway? Wait, that's near Sweden, isn't it?"

15

How to Get to Norway Without Flying

Mr. Kalman wants to take us all to REI for winter clothes, but Catalina says, "Swap, don't shop." She tweets a change of season announcement for the next Swap Stop—this one at North Hollywood Park, since school is out: *Summer is here, Winter is gone, Time to pass your warm clothes along.*

As we arrive, the tables fill up, and we have our pick of parkas, hats, gloves, and boots. Cat calculates the savings to us—more than $3,500. And to all the families who swapped today—$12,500.

Alistair holds up a red and white Rossignol ski jacket. "Cool," he says. "It's French."

Back at home, I stuff my brand-used puffy down jacket— okay, my brand-used *pink* puffy down jacket—into a duffel, roll the wool socks and not exactly long underwear I found, and tuck in the face mask and gloves.

There's an expression my mom likes to use: *Don't put the cart before the horse,* which means, basically, don't get ahead of yourself. Plan before you act. Or, in this case, before you pack. The planning part comes when you ask your mom for permission to go.

You're supposed to do that *before* you stuff a duffel.

"Sam, why are you packing winter clothes? It's August. The height of summer."

"In some parts of the world, yeah. But in others, like Argentina, it's winter."

"You're going to Argentina?"

"Nope. Someplace way to the north. Norway."

"No way."

"Norway. With an *r.*"

"No. Way. With an *n-o.*"

I try to convince her. I tell her it's part of our plan to get the amendment passed. We'll occupy the Doomsday Vault and hold the seeds hostage. We won't leave until the state legislatures sign.

Mom is dubious. She doesn't see how a seed vault north of the Arctic Circle could matter to a bunch of states six thousand miles away.

"Those seeds are the most valuable things on Earth. They're like a backup hard drive for all the files we'll need to survive if the world's crops fail."

"Aren't there soldiers guarding that place?"

"A few."

"Armed?"

"Everybody in Svalbard is armed. Polar bears outnumber humans there."

"*Polar bears?* Like I said, *no way*."

Here's where I manipulate my mom. She's dead set against me going, but I know what she needs to hear in order to change her mind.

"You come too."

She looks at me.

"It can get really cold in Svalbard. I might need you."

I don't really need my mom to come, but if it gets her to say yes . . .

"Honey, I can't leave town. I'm too busy with work."

Then she thinks.

"Mr. Kalman is going?"

"And Betty. So that's two people over eighteen. *Way* over."

"Maybe Sadie could go with you too."

"She can't, Mom. She's leaving soon to do outreach with the homeless in Providence."

Mom thinks.

"How will I know you're okay?"

"Because you'll hear about it. The whole world will."

"And . . ."

"And I'll text every day."

138

★

She looks at me.

"I mean call. I'll call every day. If there's a signal."

• • •

If you go on Google Maps and enter the starting point as the NoHo Senior Arts Colony and the destination as the Svalbard Global Seed Vault, it says *Sorry, your search appears to be outside our current coverage area for transit.* But a nice map of the world shows up, with a star in North Hollywood, California, and a bull's-eye on an ice-covered island in the Barents Sea.

There *are* flights available, with only three stops. The fastest itinerary will get you there in eighteen hours. If they're on time.

Suppose you don't want to fly. Your only other option is to travel by ship. Cruise ships leave from Alaska and travel through the Northwest Passage, but they're very expensive. We might be able to catch an oil tanker from Texas through the Gulf of Mexico, around the Florida panhandle, up the Atlantic to the Norwegian Sea, but the last time an oil tanker made the Texas-to-Norway run was 1985. Besides, it would be pretty hypocritical if we took an oil tanker to Svalbard in our fight against fossil fuels.

Mr. Kalman comes up with a solution. "I have to warn you, it involves impersonating a school group."

"We're school-age kids. What's so hard about that?"

"You'll pretend to be a group of science students who have

139
★

won their statewide competition in oceanography. That's our cover."

"Are we going to have to pass a quiz?" Alistair says. "Because if so, I'm out."

"No quiz. Just act the part. I've made a deal with the captain of the *Roald Amundsen,* a science cruise ship named for the Norwegian explorer who discovered the Northwest Passage from Europe to Alaska. The vessel is on her way back from Antarctica and will be at the Port of San Diego in two days."

"You bought us cabins on a cruise, Mr. Kalman? That's so generous."

"Not exactly. The *Roald Amundsen* is headed back for its annual maintenance. They have a skeletal crew and need workers to clean the ship."

"What job will *you* be doing?" I ask.

"The *Roald Amundsen* has two Jacuzzis, an infinity pool, and a sauna with a view of the sea. You'll find me in one of those locations. Or in the science center, viewing the video that displays images from the Blue Eye, the ship's underwater drone."

"That doesn't sound like work."

"I'm just the chaperone. You're the science students. Consider it like a semester at sea. With serious work detail."

"What kind of cleaning?"

"There are three hundred and seventy-five toilets on board. I promised the captain they'd be spotless by San Francisco."

"One question," Alistair says. "Do they have a five-star chef on the ship?"

"Normally, yes. But she's on vacation. You will take over in the galley."

"How long will we be afloat, sir?"

"Nineteen days."

"Aye-aye. Breakfast, lunch, and dinner. That's forty-seven meals."

"Fifty-seven meals," Catalina corrects.

"I'll bring my recipe book. And a few supplies."

"There's something else we'll have to do. Convince the crew to land us on Jan Mayen Island. But you can't reveal why. If the Norwegian government finds out that they willingly abetted our siege of the seed bank, the crew will be tried for mutiny against the Crown."

"Will they lose their rank?"

"Their rank, yes. And possibly their lives."

• • •

I go over to Alistair's house to help him pack. He's got one duffel full of clothes and another full of —

"Kitchen supplies?"

"We're going on an Arctic cruise, Sam. The ship's cook won't be there, so we're pretty much on our own for food prep. I want to be prepared."

He tosses in a bunch of odd gadgets I've never seen.

"What's that?" I ask, looking at a piece of wood shaped like a bowling pin.

"Spurtle. You use it to stir large quantities of oatmeal."

"And these?" They're bands of thick silver foil with Velcro at the ends.

"Cake strips. You wrap the pans with them to protect the edges from burning."

I watch as he hoists a heavy appliance into the bottom of the bag.

"You trying to sink the ship?"

"That's my Ninja air fryer. Makes the crispiest french fries you'll ever eat. Wait 'til you taste them with my roasted pepper and shallot aioli."

He tosses in a set of metal tips and plastic bags.

"Piping set. A dessert should look as good as it tastes."

He adds a wand with a mini propeller at the bottom.

"Immersion blender. Cordless."

Another heavy pot. "Dutch oven for sourdough bread."

Finally this scary-looking thing that looks like a gas pump crossed with a glue gun.

142
★

"What on Earth is that?" I say.

"My Bernzomatic TS8000. A high-intensity blowtorch. It's how I crust the top of my crème brûlée."

He sets it inside, zips up the duffel, and starts to hand it to me.

"On second thought, you grab one end, I'll grab the other. A guy could get hurt carrying this load on his own."

And yeah, it's heavy. But I'll admit I'm curious to try his Ninja french fries.

• • •

Mr. Kalman, by contrast, packs unbelievably light. His backpack looks like something a little kid would carry—for their doll. I'd be surprised if he could fit more than three pairs of underwear in there.

"Mr. Kalman, you realize we could be away for three weeks."

"I've learned how to travel light, Sam. You never know when my next voyage will be my last."

"Oh, please," Betty says, pushing her walker to the curb. Behind her, Zoe is wrangling a ginormous suitcase on skateboard-type wheels. "You're just trying to make the rest of us feel like we overpacked."

We all stare at her suitcase. I'm surprised it even fits in her apartment.

"Are Zoe's things combined with yours in there?" Mr. Kal-man asks.

"Zoe has her own backpack."

Which Zoe holds up—a small Swiss Army backpack about the size of mine.

"So the move to Norway, for you, is permanent?"

"Listen, Avi. I haven't been on a cruise since Mel and I crossed the Atlantic. I plan to travel in comfort."

"We're going to need another Uber," Mr. Kalman says.

• • •

On the train to San Diego, we check out the website for the *Roald Amundsen*. It's operated by Hurtigruten and is one of two hybrid cruise ships. It can take five hundred passengers, a small number for a cruise ship. But the *Amundsen* is no ordinary cruise ship. Passengers who travel on it don't just see the sights; they do science along the way. It's got an underwater drone, a science center with microscopes, VR goggles, and a full-height LED screen in the lobby—fifty-one feet tall and twenty-one feet wide. Now *that's* a big screen. The "Polar Outside cabins" are, and I quote from the website, "decorated in a modern style that matches the rest of the ship, featuring TVs and en suite bathrooms" (which we'll be having to clean). It's also one of the only cruise ships that is committed to protecting the environment. "The first cruise line in the world to remove all single-use plastic from our ship."

Mr. Kalman was right about the amenities: an infinity pool, a sauna, and a pair of Jacuzzis. There's even a jogging track around B deck.

Our Uber drops us at the Embarcadero, and we make our way to the Hornblower pier. The *Amundsen* is the second cruise ship docked there. I recognize the blue, white, and red flag of Norway.

But before we can board, we have to show our passports to the U.S. Customs people.

"What is the purpose of your trip to Norway?" a uniformed officer asks.

"Oh, see, we're just a bunch of science geeks going to occu—"

"Observe . . . a polar bear," Zoe says while Catalina covers Alistair's mouth.

He looks at the customs officer, who stares him down. I'm hoping this guy has a sense of humor.

"Good luck with that," he says, and waves us on.

"Alistair!"

"I know, I know. It almost slipped. I get nervous around uniforms."

We head up the gangway. Captain Nils Knudsen is waiting for us at the top. He's wearing—you guessed it—a captain's cap, black, with a gold anchor stitched to the front. And he has a sea captain's beard, black and white and full from a long time without shaving. If I'd been to Antarctica, I'd probably stop shaving too.

Except I'm not old enough to grow a beard.

"Welcome to the *Roald Amundsen*," the captain says. "And congratulations on taking first prize in the state science fair."

"Just don't ask us too many questions, sir," Alistair says. "We're letting our brains rest."

He tells us he'll give us one day off, but tomorrow he'll launch the Blue Eye and show us "the wonders — and the worries — of the sea. Come, explore the ship."

A five-hundred-passenger state-of-the-art high-tech hybrid cruise ship all to ourselves! I've got to hand it to Mr. Kalman. He knows how to travel in style.

Soon we're backing out of the slip, and soon after that we're leaving San Diego Bay. Our first stop: San Francisco, 530 nautical miles away. According to the captain, the *Amundsen* cruises at a speed of 15 knots, so we'll be there in a day and a half.

That's half a day to relax. One day to clean 375 toilets.

At least the tickets were free.

16

The Blue Eye

If we were feeling anxious about lying to a ship's captain while planning to kidnap the world's emergency seed supply; if we were having second thoughts about amending the Constitution to stop global warming; if we were worried about all the people who might become jobless, homeless, or hungry because of our action; if we were getting seasick already and wishing we weren't climate warriors after all, all we needed was to see the world through the Blue Eye.

The Blue Eye is the underwater drone camera on the *Roald Amundsen*. It can dive to a depth of a thousand feet and send back video to the LED wall in the lobby. It can show you in high-def the beauty of the sea. And it can show you in that same high-def the hard truth that most of us ignore.

The tangle of floating plastic in San Francisco Bay, like a man-made sea monster, its scraggly hair a trap for sea lions and fish.

A bottlenose dolphin with a Coke bottle in its mouth.

Fish tangled in six-pack holders.

So much plastic is floating by, it takes a second to recognize the different kinds. Coffee cup lids. Plastic spoons. Chess pieces. Plastic bags and plastic lighters. Cell phones and baby bottles and disposable pens. Straws, food wrappers, cigarette butts. Flash drives and letters from plastic keyboards, plastic glasses and plastic goggles.

"It grows ten times larger every ten years," the captain explains. "Some of the plastic is more than fifty years old. Most of it you can't see, even with the Blue Eye."

With the remote control, he moves the arm of the Blue Eye. It scoops up a water sample. Later, when the drone surfaces and we look at the water under the microscope, we see bits of microplastic swirling around.

"There's plastic in rivers, plastic in lakes, plastic in the stomachs of animals and in the bloodstreams of human beings."

We all stand there, shocked and silent.

"We have to get rid of it," Jaesang finally says.

"It would take hundreds of years."

"So? If we don't start now, it could take thousands."

Captain Knudsen looks at us. "You care about the planet," he says.

148
★

"We do," Alistair says. "As a matter of fact, we wrote an amen—"

Catalina shoves her thumb up Alistair's armpit—his top tickle zone. We told him not to tell. We warned him that if the captain finds out about our real mission, that could be the end.

"We care a lot because we're trying to get a master's degree in science," I say. "Someday."

"A noble goal. Your voyage on the *Amundsen* should help."

He turns and heads back to the bridge.

Alistair shrugs. "I forgot. It won't happen again."

• • •

We dock at Pier 39 in San Francisco. Alistair takes over as tour guide, pointing out the sights around the pier: the restaurants with neon lights, the artists selling their crafts, the crowded souvenir stands.

"Do you have kids, Captain?"

"Nieces and nephews, Alistair. They've never been to San Francisco. I'd like to buy them a souvenir."

"Maybe they'd like a scented candle. Or a Golden Gate Bridge key chain. Or . . . a caricature of you."

He nods to a row of artists, sketches hanging from a clothesline behind them.

"No, thanks," he says.

"Well, I'm going to poke around. I'll meet you guys at Ghirardelli's."

"I'm going with Alistair," Mr. Kalman says. "Maybe I'll find a *New York Times.*"

We walk on, and I notice that Captain Knudsen has his eye on something else. A block away there's a homeless encampment. Tents and shopping carts and scraggly dogs on scraps of carpet. People wearing old clothes. Plastic bags bulging with aluminum cans.

"Why are so many people living on the streets?" he asks.

"They're homeless," I say.

"The city doesn't give them shelter?"

Now that I think about it, it's strange to see so many homeless near all the souvenirs for sale.

"Don't you have homeless people in Norway?"

"We do. But not so many as this all in one place. We have centers where they can find food, a bed, medical care, and clothing. In Norway, Sam, we have what you might call welfare capitalism. The essential things are free."

"How does the government pay for that?"

"Taxes, of course. But also from our industries. Norway exports ninety percent of the oil and gas in the European Union."

Great. We're posing as a science class on our way to Norway on a Norwegian science ship, but secretly we're using the captain to get close enough to Svalbard so we can kidnap the seeds in the Global Seed Vault and hold them hostage until eleven more states in America ratify an amendment that could force such a huge change in the world's economies that Norway's oil and gas industry will go bankrupt and there'll be homeless people on the streets of Oslo. That's what my mom calls thinking it through.

I just lost my appetite for a hot fudge sundae.

But Alistair still has his. Later, he comes rushing over to our booth at Ghirardelli's with a plastic bag in one hand and a newspaper in the other.

"Guys," he says, "check this out. We made the *New York Times*."

He drops the paper on the table. I catch a glimpse of us holding up a JUST SAY YES banner in Baton Rouge, but before I can read the whole headline, Catalina slaps the paper with her open palm and scoops it up, leaning back in the booth to read aloud.

"Science Nerds Win State Prize. A group of dedicated science students at Reed Middle School have taken top prize in an alternative energy competition. Their project" — she looks up at us, stalling, then nods and goes on — "how plants provide all the solar panels we'll ever need. 'By attaching thin wires to the leaves of oak trees,' Jaesang Lee explained, 'we were able to recharge our cell phones.'"

151
★

"That's a very innovative idea," the captain says.

"It sure is," Zoe says.

"Well, the article goes on—but look, here come our hot fudge sundaes."

I don't know how Alistair can eat his with so many angry eyes staring at him. He shrugs a silent apology, then digs in while Catalina stashes the newspaper under her leg.

I can't help it. I lean over to peek at the headline: Louisiana Ratifies Planet Amendment.

Seems like, in Louisiana, they're worried about the long term after all.

★ The Road to Ratification ★

17

Storm Warning

Two days later, back on board, the captain tells us to prepare for rough seas. We'll be refueling in Astoria, Oregon, a port town near the mouth of the Columbia River. But first we have to cross the bar. The bar is where the Columbia collides with the Pacific Ocean. When the two bodies of water smash together during a storm, they can make waves up to forty feet high.

"Its nickname," the captain tells us, "is the Graveyard of the Pacific. More than two thousand ships have gone down there."

Terrified, I look at Jaesang and Alistair.

The captain smiles. "The worst storms usually don't form until winter."

Usually?

Jaesang asks to see the weather instruments on board. The captain leads us to the bridge.

If your idea of heaven is being stuck overnight at a Radio-

Shack, if you know the difference between a DSC and a NAV-TEX receiver, know what an INMARASAT signal is and where you can receive it, or why a polar-bound vessel like this one would need an HF radio and what SSAS stands for, then you'd geek out in the bridge of the *Roald Amundsen*. Aside from all the cool navigational instruments, state-of-the-art video screens, dual swivel captain's chairs that no self-respecting gamer would *ever* get out of even if they did run out of Cheez-Its, it has the most advanced onboard weather devices that money—and at 220 million dollars, I mean *a lot of money*—can buy.

We stand there slack-jawed and stuck-eyed. The bridge has sixteen windows and a panorama view east, north, and west. We can hear the hum of the hybrid engine, the slapping of waves against the hull, and the bleep of sonar looking out for obstructions in and on the sea.

Mr. Kalman had said there'd be a skeletal crew with us. One of them is Lucy Dahlberg, Captain Knudsen's first officer. She swivels around in the first officer's chair and says hello.

Technically, only high-ranking sailors—first officer and above—are allowed on the bridge. But I've found that grownups like to bend the rules for curious kids.

"Would anyone like a seat?" Lucy Dahlberg asks, rising from her chair.

"I would," I say.

"We would," Zoe and Catalina say, tumbling into the bridge.

"I wouldn't," Alistair says. "Outside of a kitchen, I have a tendency to hit all the wrong buttons."

"Jaesang?" Captain Knudsen says.

But Jaesang is huddled over the aneroid barometer, looking worried. "The pressure is dropping, Captain. Do we have internet on board?"

"Usually."

That word again.

"Can you pull up NOAA's forecast for the eastern Pacific?" Jaesang asks. "I've got a bad feeling."

Lucy Dahlbeg moves to a computer screen next to Jaesang. She logs on, and together they study the weather map.

Zoe and Catalina swivel around and around in the twin captain's chairs.

"How do you become a ship's captain?" Catalina asks.

If I know Cat, she's dreaming of a new career.

"Well, Catalina, you've already taken the first step," says Lucy Dahlberg. "Do an internship on board a vessel. Next, you'll have to graduate from middle and high school, attend college or a maritime academy, go to grad school for a master's in maritime engineering, then get certified and credentialed as a mariner. After that it's just a matter of passing some of the most difficult licensing exams out there. Sounds easy, doesn't it?"

"No. Sounds hard. But worth it." She sits a little taller in the chair.

Then Jaesang calls over. "The jet stream has shifted. There's a tropical storm moving north by northwest from Hawaii."

"He's right," Lucy Dahlberg says. "NOAA just issued a storm warning for our region."

The captain looks at the screen, then orders us all back to our berths.

• • •

Soon we're rocking up and down, side to side, forward and back. The floor of the ship feels like silly putty. I can't walk across it without holding on to a table, a chair, or a handrail, all of them bolted down. A monster wave slams against the windows. Sea spray floods the decks. The wind sounds like a thousand breaths blowing into a thousand bottles.

Jaesang and Zoe and Catalina made it back to their rooms, but I'm worried about Mr. Kalman and Betty. I can't find Alistair, either . . . until he appears staggering toward me from the port side of the ship.

"Stay out of the bathroom, Sam," he says. "My brioche French toast just hit the wall."

He sinks to the floor, hunches over, and moans.

The boat heaves again. I start down the stairs. My hand is like dried concrete on the rail. Step. Hold. Step. Hold. Step hold.

At the bottom I sway from side to side, move past my room, where Jaesang is lying on his bed, creaking like the ship itself. I knock on Betty's door. Zoe answers, says they're okay. Then I hear Catalina's panicked voice.

"Sam, in here! Help!

It's coming from Mr. Kalman's room.

I feel queasy, but I keep going . . . get my hand on his door handle . . . and push open the door.

"Catalina?"

"In the bathroom."

I go around the corner. The first thing I see are Mr. Kalman's feet on the floor. I move closer and see him lying on his back. Catalina holds a towel to his head. The towel used to be white.

• • •

Dear Greta,

Greetings from the Roald Amundsen, location top secret. We just got slammed by a tropical storm out of Hawaii. It felt like the start of Gilligan's Island. My mom told me to pack Dramamine but I bragged, said I can take anything the ocean has to give. Next time I'm listening to my mom.

Of course, what I did to the bathroom is nothing

compared to what Mr. Kalman did. He was shaving when the first swell hit. Lucky he put his razor down in time. Unlucky the wave knocked him off his feet. His head banged into the doorframe and gave it a new paint job. He was out cold for twenty minutes, until Catalina and Sam went to check on him. When they finally showed up in the Explorer Lounge, Mr. Kalman walked in pushing Betty's walker.

We all gathered around him and asked if he was okay. With Mr. Kalman, you never know if his injuries are real or fake. One time he faked a fall in front of the Watergate Hotel. He even fooled the paramedics. But these injuries were real.

"Okay is a relative term," he said. "I'm dizzy. But I've always been hardheaded, so I'll probably survive. And thanks to Betty's generosity, I'm mobile."

This morning we woke up to blue skies, calm waters, and clean bathrooms. The crew was finally hungry again, so I made oatmeal for all. Used my secret ingredient—bananas—and added cinnamon brown sugar and a dollop of sour cream. Gently stirred with my spurtle. After breakfast, Captain Knudsen asked me if I'd like to drop out of middle school and be his personal chef on the high seas.

"I can pay you 750,000 kroner a year," he said.

I asked Siri how much is 750,000 kroner, but Catalina answered first.

"90,000 U.S. dollars," she said.

That's WAY more than minimum wage, and I'm only 12.

Mr. Kalman said if I take the job, I'll be in violation of the child labor laws.

Sam said I should go for it. Whenever can a 7th grader make that much money?

Zoe said I should turn him down and not worry about money. "You'll earn plenty as a grownup, Alistair."

My head says take the money. 750,000 kroner in your pocket is worth more than 750,000 kroner not in your pocket.

But my heart says I'd miss my friends. I told Captain Knudsen I'll think about it and get back to him in ten years.

Gotta go. We're stopping in ████████████████, today for tuna fish 'n' chips and fuel. Then we head north to ████████.

Yours from ████████████████,
Alistair

P.S. There's plastic everywhere, even in human blood.

P.P.S. We're going to take bold action to stop global warming. Keep your eye on the news.

· · ·

Days at sea, nights at sea, the *Amundsen* glides north. The weather is back to its August mood, calm and clear. At night we see an infinity of stars. It's like all the dogs in the universe swam through a river of white paint and then shook themselves off in the sky.

I think about that song my mom used to sing me when I was a little kid falling asleep.

I see the moon and the moon sees me
The moon sees somebody I want to see
God bless the moon and God bless me
And God bless the somebody I want to see.

But I doubt she can see what I see. We hear that back in L.A., there are fires raging in the San Gabriel Mountains. Even if she's looking up at the same night sky, how can my mom see stars through a dome of smoke?

On day 3, we hear of a terrible storm in Florida. Hurricane Juanito came ashore with winds over 150 miles per hour. Tallahassee was flooded, and more than a million people lost power. It's another climate tragedy, but maybe it happened for a reason. Today, Florida became the twenty-ninth state to ratify the Planet Amendment.

On day 4, I notice that Catalina and Zoe are up to something top secret. They won't tell us what it is, but it involves bedsheets, which they steal from the laundry room, and needle and thread, which they steal from Betty's luggage. I hope they're not planning to trap a polar bear.

On day 5, we cross into the Arctic Ocean. I'm by myself on the observation deck, wearing mittens now and a wool cap, watching the icy blue water, when I feel someone standing behind me. I turn and see Jaesang. The cold wind puffs up his black hair, making him look even taller, stronger.

"It's conscious, you know," he says.

"What, the sea?"

"The sea. The land. The planet."

I give him a look that says I'm not so sure.

"According to physics, matter cannot be destroyed or created, right? So if the same ingredients that make us—carbon, water, calcium, proteins—also exist in and around the Earth, and if we have consciousness, then the planet has consciousness too."

"But consciousness isn't a physical thing, Jae. It's an idea. An abstract noun."

"Born in a concrete place: the brain."

"Is a basketball conscious?"

"I like to think so. Less than a dog, maybe. Or a tree. But yeah. Everything is."

He tells me about this documentary he saw on Nat Geo, about a diver who made friends with an octopus. "He was feeling depressed."

"The man or the octopus?"

"Both. The man started diving every day near his house in South Africa. And every day he'd observe the same octopus. For a whole year he followed her, filmed her, and made friends with her. She came to trust him, Sam. An animal can't learn to trust unless it's aware."

I can see how an octopus might be conscious, but not a basketball. Still, I don't want to ruin Jaesang's Theory of All Things Being Conscious, so I keep my doubts to myself.

But when a pair of beluga whales breach the water 130 feet from the starboard side of the boat and make eye contact with us, I think maybe everything *is* conscious, and maybe those whales and the floating ice and the pelican we just saw dive for a fish, and the planet itself, all know why we're here. And I hope they're glad we've come.

We go back inside and find everyone staring up at the LED wall. A blue beacon shows us our location on the world map.

"Our route to Norway takes us from Pond Inlet northeast around Greenland to Tromsø, home of the *Amundsen*," the captain says. "We should arrive in port by Friday." Alistair and I exchange a glance. Soon, I think, we'll have to take over the ship.

"Unless you'd like to make a detour to the Global Seed Vault in Svalbard," the captain adds.

"Alistair!!!!! We told you not to tell."

"He didn't tell. The *New York Times* did."

Captain Knudsen drops a newspaper on the table. The headline reads LOUISIANA RATIFIES PLANET AMENDMENT. Beneath it is a picture of me and Alistair holding up a banner: NO MORE KATRINAS. NO MORE IDAS. JUST SAY YES.

"I picked it up in Astoria," he says. "It was a few days old."

But Zoe has her doubts. "Wait a minute. All that tells you is we marched in Baton Rouge. How'd you make the connection to Svalbard?"

The captain looks at us. He looks at Alistair.

But before we can say *Alistaaaaiiiiirrrrr* again, Mr. Kalman speaks up.

"You can direct your outrage at me, kids. I realized that our plan would never succeed without the complicity of the captain."

"It's a good thing he told me, too," Captain Knudsen says. "Otherwise you would have had to commandeer the ship, face charges of mutiny, and likely been sentenced to twenty years in Tromsø Prison. That's no place for children."

Suddenly I feel very afraid. "Are you going to turn us in, Captain Knudsen?"

"I am going to help you. We all are."

Members of the skeletal crew come forward, including Lucy Dahlberg.

"We'll drop anchor off the coast of Spitsbergen," the captain continues. "I will radio the Norwegian Home Guard to say you are a group of schoolchildren come to study the Arctic. I will request a tour of the seed bank for you. You will kayak to shore. There's a nature trail from the cove up to the plateau where the seed bank sits. Locals often lead hiking tours there. You will hike up to the entrance, but Mr. Kalman and Miss Betty will pretend to be an old married couple who get 'lost' and require assistance from the Guard. Perhaps a fake injury . . ."

"He's great at those," I say, nodding toward Mr. Kalman.

"He's good at real ones too," Betty says, resting her hand on Mr. Kalman's arm.

"That will draw them away from the entrance just as you go inside. The rest, I'm afraid, is up to you. I can't risk jail time, but I can facilitate your capture of the vault because, children, I support your cause."

He looks out the tall glass windows at the sea lions and the sea beyond.

"This route we've sailed, through some of the most pristine, untouched landscapes on Earth, gives me a profound connection to nature. The animals we see—above water and below—are all the proof I need that the planet has a soul and must be saved. Now get some food—which Alistair has prepared—and some rest, which you'll need for the kayaking.

"Tomorrow we take Svalbard."

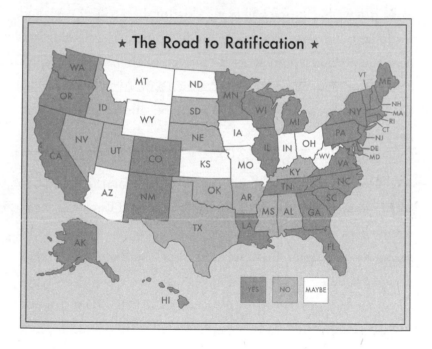

18

Perpetual Repercussion

In August, 150 miles from the North Pole, the sun looks like a pale yellow beach ball being slow-motion tossed back and forth, east and west. You might see it dip behind a floating iceberg, but it's always somewhere in the sky. Night never comes. It's light out at ten p.m. Still light out at two a.m. Even at five, when the captain's steward wakes us. We pull off our sleep shades and rise from bed.

Today, we take Svalbard.

Our resolve comes from outrage: the island of plastic in San Francisco Bay, the sea lions suffering from cancer, massive wildfires and floods, the incredibly crappy job humans have done caring for the planet. First, we were shocked; then, we got mad; now, we're here.

Our strength comes from Alistair's 750,000 kroner oatmeal. A banana scent rises from steaming bowls. The dining room is quiet except for blowing on spoons and, later, scraping the bottoms of bowls.

After breakfast we bundle up in our new-old clothes from the summer-winter swap. My pink parka isn't exactly camouflage, but it'll keep me warm on the icy water.

We meet up on C deck. The crew lowers kayaks into the water, then lowers us into the kayaks — two at a time — and when we're all loaded, Captain Knudsen guides us into Adventfjorden, the narrow inlet that runs to the bottom of the mountain where the seed vault stands.

It's six a.m., but Zoe is wide-awake. We share a boat, but she's not paddling. She's too busy pointing out birds.

"Guys, look — an Arctic tern. And there, on the rocks, those are Canada geese. And there in the water, common eiders."

We float by a row of black and white ducks with yellow bills.

"Know why those slopes are so green?" she asks.

"Sunlight?" I guess.

"Fertilizer. Look up."

We do, and there on the ice-free cliffs above we see hundreds of tiny black and white birds.

"Little auks make a lot of poop. It fertilizes the plants that feed the geese that feed the Arctic foxes. A perfect balance."

It's as if Zoe has a sixth sense for the living things on Earth.

We paddle closer to the shore. Zoe calls out more birds. Fulmar. Skua. Kittiwake. Puffin. Glaucous gulls. Funny-looking birds with funny-sounding names.

We paddle past two seals lounging on an iceberg. They have long beards and droopy eyes.

"No closer than that," the captain warns. He widens the curve of our line of boats. We paddle softly toward shore.

Toward, but not all the way onto the shore because, about a hundred yards away, walking like he owns the island, we spot a lone polar bear.

Everyone gets quiet. We've seen them on Nat Geo, in documentaries, and in pictures on the internet. We've seen them in books too. I remember in first grade Ms. McCloud read us *The Three Snow Bears.* She unrolled a clean white carpet over the stained blue rug where we always sat for story time. *Today, we're going to the Arctic,* she said. And she read us a version of "Goldilocks and the Three Bears," only it was Aloo-ki and three polar bears. I remember wondering why the polar bears needed sweaters.

The illustrations were cool, but there's nothing like seeing a polar bear in the wild. It takes your voice away. Even Zoe stops calling out the names of birds. The polar bear eyes us, pads along the ground, and wades into the cold sea. A wave ripples out; our kayaks sway.

"Don't worry," the captain tells us, "his appetite for humans is low this time of year."

I wouldn't want to meet him in spring.

As soon as the bear is out of sight, we beach our kayaks, wave goodbye to the captain, and start on the mile hike along a switchback trail up to the vault. Jaesang and Zoe practically carry Betty while Alistair and I guide Mr. Kalman. A sign at the trailhead says SVALBARD HIKING TOURS MEET HERE. CAUTION: POLAR BEAR CROSSING AHEAD. We start up the trail.

About halfway up, we fall into a heavy mist. We can hear but can't see the birds. We can smell but can't see the flowers growing from the cliff. We can barely see each other now.

It's one careful step at a time, until we reach the top, and the mist fades away, and a flash of gray and white darts past: a family of Arctic foxes. The larger ones — I'm guessing it's the mother and father — are ripping a dead bird to shreds, eating it raw. One of the younger foxes sneaks up, tries to steal a piece for himself, but a parent snarls at him. He skitters away.

Then the other young fox creeps up from the other side, steals the same piece of meat, and runs to join his brother or sister.

Zoe tells us that Arctic foxes are famous for their survival skills. "Once, a young fox crossed the ice from here all the way to

Canada. She walked over two thousand miles in just seventy-five days."

The pups, she tells us, learn to fend for themselves early on.

When the ground levels out, we practice posing as kids on a field trip, which is kind of what we are, and Mr. Kalman and Betty rehearse as a married couple, which is hilarious because already they're bickering over how bad the fake injury should be.

"It should cause me to grunt," Mr. Kalman says.

"Scream," Betty says. "A broken leg at the very least."

Zoe tells me not to worry. Betty was an actress when she was young. She played comedic roles on Broadway.

"Mr. Kalman can act too," I tell her. "He can fool a hospital."

Alistair, though, has probably the hardest role to play. He pulls a blond girl's wig from his backpack.

Mr. Kalman looks confused. "What are you doing?"

"There's a satellite dish at Svalbard. If the guards watch *MasterChef Junior*, they'll know who I really am. It could compromise the mission, so I picked up this wig in San Francisco."

He puts on the wig.

He turns to Zoe. "Lipstick?"

Zoe turns Alistair's lips an electric shade of pink. Mr. Kalman and Betty peel off from the group.

We trek up the hill, Alistair carrying the backpack with

snacks and supplies, Zoe carrying a backpack of her own with something big and bulging in there. Twenty minutes later Mr. Kalman and Betty veer onto a side trail. Up ahead, we see a huge rectangle sticking out of a mountain, like a concrete robot poking out from its lair. The mouth is a heavy steel door. The forehead is a wall of blue and green glass lit from within. It looks like someone trapped the northern lights in a giant glass box.

The Svalbard Global Seed Vault.

We stand there, awed by the power of the building, the beauty of its sculpture. Catalina read up on it while we were at sea. "The light sculpture is called *Perpetual Repercussion,*" she says. "The artist, Dyveke Sanne, wanted people to think about reflection. The sculpture reflects the northern lights, which makes it beautiful. But it's also a shattered mirror, so it makes us think about what we're doing to the planet. Beauty or destruction, what will each of us make? The seeds inside are humanity's last hope."

She steps toward the Norwegian soldier standing guard, shotgun hanging from his shoulder by a leather strap.

"Good morning," she says, "I'm Catalina Gladys Consuela Martinez, captain of our school's nature club. These are our students come all the way from Los Angeles."

The heavy steel door opens, and a woman steps out to greet us. She's tall, with blond hair and a yellow construction hat. She wears glasses and an ID badge: ASTRID LARSEN.

"Welcome to the Svalbard Global Seed Vault. I am Astrid, your guide. You've made such a long journey. Are you excited for your visit?"

We look at one another and nod like eager schoolchildren, which in a way we are.

"Before we go inside, let me ask you, why seeds? Why spend seven hundred and fifty million kroner each year on a giant freezer for seeds?"

"Seeds are awesome," Alistair says.

"Yes. But most countries have their own vaults. Why have a backup here?"

"In case of global disaster," I say. "An asteroid or a nuclear war."

"And to maintain diversity," Zoe says.

"Exactly. We're the backup of the backups. Twenty years from now, many crops will have failed from drought or climate change. Farmers may need to go back in time to a variety of seed that is heartier, can grow in a harsher climate. Those seeds may be gone from Nigeria or Nebraska, Peru or Lebanon—but their backup copies will be here."

"Food forever," Alistair says.

"Food forever," Astrid says.

Just then a hysterical woman comes racing up to the entrance —pushing her walker, which would have blown our cover if she

172
★

wasn't such a good actress. "Please, can you help me? My husband has fallen on the trail. He can't get up."

It's Betty. She's so in character that for a second even Zoe doesn't recognize her.

Astrid turns to the young soldier, tells him to go for help, she'll be fine on her own with the children.

He nods and walks off with Betty—and his gun.

"I think it's a broken ankle," we hear Betty say.

We follow Astrid inside.

She leads us down a long, wide concrete tube, its walls coated in ice.

"Fog breath," Alistair says, breathing a white mist from his mouth.

"Me too," says Jaesang.

Astrid explains that the vault was dug 350 meters into the mountainside. Even if global warming melts the ground ice outside, the seeds in here will remain in permafrost.

"If we lose power, the natural temperature inside will stay at zero degrees Celsius. As long as it stays cold, the seeds are safe."

We go through another door, following the tunnel deeper underground. Colder too.

"We have nearly a million unique seed packets from 233 countries, with about 500 seeds in each packet. The total number of seeds in the collection so far is 560 million—150,000 types of wheat and rice, 80,000 kinds of barley, 35,000 kinds of maize, 15,000 varieties of peanuts, 4,000 lettuces, 3,000 tomatoes, and 3,700 types of potatoes. Have you ever had Mormon tea?"

We all shake our heads.

"How about giant hyssop, wall rocket, bastard cabbage, or skullcap?"

We try not to crack up at these funny names.

"I didn't think so," Astrid says. "No one, not even a botanist, can name all the seeds in Svalbard. Anyone like to cook?"

We all look at Alistair.

"*She* does," I say.

"But just as a hobby," Alistair says. He's still worried she'll recognize him.

"You could scan all the recipes ever written and still not find all the varieties of food grown from the seeds in this vault. Even the ones that are no longer cultivated are saved from extinction here."

I ask her if any of the countries has ever had to take their seeds out.

"Yes," she says. "During the Syrian Civil War, scientists in Aleppo evacuated eighty percent of their backup seeds to Svalbard. In those boxes were drought- and heat-resistant varieties of wheat, fava beans, chickpeas, and the world's largest collection of barley seed. If the Aleppo seed bank got bombed or even lost

174
★

power to its freezers, those seeds could be lost forever. They decided to build a new seed bank in Lebanon, and they came to us for our first withdrawal."

There's an expression in English—*getting cold feet.* It describes that feeling of all of a sudden being unsure about something that, a minute ago, you were 100 percent determined to do. People get cold feet when they're about to jump out of a plane or zip-line across a huge crevasse or, so I've heard, get married.

Right now, we're all getting cold feet. How can we take seeds as hostages when they might have to feed people in a war zone? Or all of humanity in a climate catastrophe?

We go through another door and then another, and past each door you can feel the temperature dropping, until it's not figurative cold feet we're getting, but literal ones. Multiple body parts are freezing in here. Even snot freezes.

"Catalina," I say, "did your snot freeze?"

"Yeah. Yours?"

"Yeah."

"Benny could never survive here," Zoe says. "Lizards can't live below forty-five degrees."

"How long you think *we* can?" I say.

Astrid tells us we won't stay long, but she wants to show us the actual vault. She waves her badge in front of a sensor. Another steel door opens.

"This is vault number two. As you can see, it's nearly full."

We're in a room way colder than the cold room at Costco. Rows of metal shelves make aisles of the open floor. They're filled with boxes, sealed and stacked two high.

"It's like the United Nations, with each country represented by their seeds. Here you have North Korea"—she points to a red box with the words DRK PEOPLE'S REPUBLIC OF KOREA written on its side—"back to back with the United States. No politics, just preparation."

"How long will this place last?" Jaesang asks.

"The seed vault was built to last two hundred years, the maximum under Norway's building code. But its inner structure —where we are now—is encased in a mountain, and that will last ten thousand years."

She turns to Zoe. "Where are your ancestors from?"

"Russia on my mom's side. Lebanon on my dad's."

"In 1903, when your great-grandmother was making borscht for the family, there were probably two hundred and eighty-five varieties of beets she could choose from. Today there are about fifteen. Ninety-four percent of the cultivars are gone."

She turns to Catalina. "And you?"

"My great-grandmother made papas a la Huancauna. Creamy, cheesy potatoes. She lived in Peru."

"We've collected more than seventeen thousand individual

tuber seeds from Peru. Peruvian potatoes are the most nutritious in the world. Did you know that NASA is experimenting with them for growing on Mars?"

Catalina smiles.

"My great-grandma had a recipe for pear upside-down cake," Alistair says. "It calls for Ansault pears, but I can never find them in a market."

"And you never will. We've lost more than twenty-six hundred pear varieties since the 1800s. There are only three hundred left."

She turns to Jaesang. "What does your family like to eat?"

"In-N-Out," he says. "But also Korean barbecue and rice."

"Here at Svalbard we have one hundred twenty thousand varieties of rice. Just in case."

It's been about forty-five minutes since we entered the vault. On our way back out, before we reach the main door, I nudge Zoe, who nudges Catalina, who nudges Alistair, who turns to Astrid and says, "I'm sorry, Astrid, but I'll need your badge."

19

We Take 500,000,000 Hostages

"Why would I give you my badge?"

"Because if you don't . . ."

Alistair reaches into his backpack and pulls out his Bernzomatic TS8000. There's a whoosh and a flash of blue light as he fires up the blowtorch.

"It'll break my heart, but I'll start burning seeds."

She stares at him, wondering if this kid is serious. He doesn't flinch.

She hands him her badge. Alistair passes it to me; I pass it to Jaesang, who passes it to Catalina, who passes it to Zoe.

"Now your radio, please."

She hands him her radio.

"You are committing a serious crime," she says. "It can only end in your arrest and incarceration in Tromsø Prison."

"A risk we're willing to take," I say.

"But why? You're just children."

"No one else seems to *really* care about climate change," Catalina says.

"We're this close to doing something that could save the planet," Jaesang says.

Alistair tells her about our amendment to the Constitution. "It'll ban all fossil fuels."

"It'll make plastic illegal," I say.

"And pollution a crime," Catalina says.

"And end cruelty to animals," Zoe says.

"If it passes, it'll set an example for the world, so that no country ever has to make another withdrawal from here again."

We look at her. She looks at us.

"What's your demand?"

"There are ten states that haven't voted. If we don't get nine of them to vote yes by this Friday, the amendment dies. But if we do, it becomes a part of the U.S. Constitution. It'll be a game changer for the planet."

"How can I help?"

"Let the Norwegian press know we're here. Tell them why."

She looks at us . . . Zoe and Catalina and Jaesang in their fierce stance by the front door. Me in my pink parka and Alistair in his blond wig, wielding a blowtorch.

"I'll need my radio back," she says.

179
★

Alistair hesitates. He hands her the radio. We all watch her as she presses the talk button and speaks in Norwegian. We hear the words *Svalbardposten. Barn. Pressen. Ja.* And *blåsebrenner.* The radio crackles, then cuts off.

Astrid hands it back to Alistair. "They're sending a crew to film you. They'll upload the feed to CNN."

"Thank you," Alistair says.

Now we wait.

Zoe and Catalina turn to Astrid. "How do you clean the glass?" Zoe says.

"Which glass?"

"In the tower. *Perpetual Repercussion.*"

"Window washers come once a year. They walk along the roof and rappel down from the top. Why?"

"Just curious," they say.

An hour later the radio crackles. Alistair presses the talk button.

"This is Alistair Martin. Over."

"Mr. Martin, I am Arild Olsen, reporter for the *Svalbard-posten.* We are outside and would like to interview you. Please, come out."

"No. You come in. But I'm warning you, no funny stuff, or we start burning seeds."

"You have my word."

He gives Cat his blåsebrenner—blowtorch—and tells her and Zoe to stand by. He asks me and Jaesang to be his bodyguards.

We wave Astrid's ID in front of the scanner. The door opens. The reporter and his camera operator come in. Then we shut the door.

I turn to Alistair and take off his wig. Jaesang wipes away his lipstick.

"Be yourself, Alistair," we say. "Be the warrior within."

He nods and turns to the press.

They film him talking about climate change and the failure of adults to do anything meaningful about it. He talks about our fears of a horrible future or, worse, none at all. He says kids across the planet have felt anxious and frustrated. But now we're mad.

"We won't stay in our seats, go to our rooms, be seen and not heard ever again. We're coming for you—corporations that pollute, governments that let them, grownups who are too scared to fight back. We're not scared. Tell them in Wyoming, tell them in West Virginia. Tell them in Arizona, and in Missouri, and in Montana. Tell them in Iowa and tell them in Ohio. Tell them all to ratify. Our Planet Amendment is our last peaceful act. If it fails, we'll fight a new kind of war. For our own survival."

We escort them out.

And we wait.

We wait . . . and we get cold. We wait . . . and we get hungry. Alistair packed his blowtorch, but he forgot to pack food.

"Did you guys bring food?" we ask Zoe and Catalina.

They shake their heads no.

We look at Astrid.

"It's the Doomsday Vault," she says. "What do you think?"

We wait while she and Catalina and Zoe go down the corridor, into a side room, and come back with energy bars and water.

We eat.

"Is there a TV or a computer with internet?" I ask.

She leads us into a small security room. She turns on a computer screen, logs on to CNN, and we see Alistair's face on-screen.

Anderson Cooper is talking. "This isn't the first time this young man, Alistair Martin, has been out front in the fight against climate change. He's the same twelve-year-old boy who was arrested earlier this year in Portland, Oregon, for stopping a freight train carrying oil from the tar sands of Canada."

We can't help it. We cheer for him. Alistair's shoulders bunch up in a modest shrug.

"The question is, will this seizure of the Svalbard Seed Vault have any influence on the voting? Let's go to John King at the Magic Wall."

They cut to John King next to CNN's Magic Wall. It shows a slicker CNN version of our Road to Ratification map.

"Well, Anderson, my sources at the statehouse in Topeka tell me that Kansas just voted yes."

He taps the state of Kansas. It turns green.

We cheer again.

And we wait some more.

It's past midnight in Svalbard. It must be below 30 degrees in here. We huddle together in the security room, hoping we can keep warm until morning. Catalina is on my right, Zoe on my left. I've never been so glad to be stuck between girls.

• • •

When I wake up the next morning, I look around for Astrid, but she's gone.

"Guys, we let Astrid get away."

We jump up, fan out, and search for her. But ten minutes later she comes walking back up the corridor.

"The bathroom is down the hall if anyone needs to go."

We all do. We take turns.

The day creeps by. We keep checking the screen. Nine states still haven't voted.

The second night feels even colder than the first. I worry about Mr. Kalman and Betty. Did they find a place to stay? Are they warm?

We nestle into the security room and watch a YouTube that Alistair wants to show us. This time it's not about the depressing impacts of climate change. This time it's about hope for a different way of living.

"These are the Earthships I was telling you about," Alistair says. "This architect has been building them in the desert of New Mexico. They're literally made from trash."

We watch, and we learn that it really is possible to build a 100 percent sustainable home. Cool air from underground can lower the inside temperature by 40 degrees in summer. Warm air trapped by the rubber tires in the walls can keep it comfortable in winter.

"It's always seventy degrees inside these houses," the narrator says. "Each one has its own greenhouse, where you can grow all the fruits and vegetables you need."

We fall asleep dreaming of a future in solar-powered Hobbit homes.

• • •

Around nine o'clock the next morning, the radio crackles again. "Astrid?" a voice calls. It sounds like the reporter from the *Svalbardposten*.

We hand her the radio. We hear something fast and loud and urgent. But we don't understand it because it's in Norwegian.

"He says we should come outside. He says there's something we'll want to see."

• • •

At the front door, Alistair reaches for the handle but looks back at me. I'm scared that on the other side of the door we'll find the police and citizens of Longyearbyen all armed with their shotguns, come to arrest us for kidnapping Astrid and five hundred million seeds.

I wave Astrid's security badge in front of the scanner. The heavy bolt is thrown back, and Jaesang muscles open the door. Daylight and cold August air flow in. I see Betty next to Mr. Kalman and the armed guard, Mr. Kalman still acting like the Tourist with the Twisted Ankle. I notice a bandage around his leg.

Over the top of his head, I see movement on the horizon. A flotilla of boats — there must be more than a hundred of them — are sailing into the fjord below. The sky looks like it's full of colorful birds, but they're really flags from different countries of the world, all waving from the masts of boats below. Flags from Denmark, Norway, Finland, Sweden; Iceland, Ireland, Britain; the Netherlands, Belgium, Germany, and France. There's one boat from Russia. Several from Canada. One from Estonia. The sea doesn't look big enough to hold all these boats.

Maybe they're coast guard ships from countries that have made deposits here, come to defend their seeds. Like Astrid said, the only nations that can make a withdrawal are the ones who made a deposit. The seeds are like money—worth more because they could be the key to survival during famine, war, flood, or drought. They're not about to let a group of kid climate activists threaten their future.

Alistair takes a look at the armada. "Guys, we're in for it now," he says. "Some of the flags . . . their countries have the death penalty."

And then we see a line of people marching over the ridge between the seed vault and the sea. They look like soldiers about to storm the castle, but instead of longbows, truncheons, and bayonets, they're carrying banners, and as they march closer, I start to see words: SAVE THE SOIL . . . SAVE THE AIR . . . SAVE THE PLANET. They march toward us, a mass of bright jackets and colorful signs. It's mostly kids, but also grownups, moms, dads, grandparents, and teenagers. Kids from Norway, Denmark, Sweden, Germany, the Netherlands, Britain, and France. From Spain and Italy and Russia. It's a wave of climate warriors, and at the center, in front, I see one face that's recognized all over the world.

Alistair's eyes pop. His face turns so red you can't see his freckles.

"Greta?" he says.

Greta Thunberg steps forward. She's standing right in front of us.

"Hello, Alistair," she says. "I got your letters. I brought some support."

"But . . . how'd you get here so fast? We only got on CNN two days ago."

"Alistair, in your letters you wrote the name of the ship, the *Roald Amundsen*. I tracked you on marinevesseltraffic.com. When I saw you enter the Northwest Passage, I guessed your plan. And I got some of my Instagram followers to come join you. We've been tracking you for days."

We look out at the great and growing crowd of protesters. Someone hands Greta a bullhorn, and she speaks into it.

"To the United States, the United Nations, and the united people of our planet, we are here in solidarity with a band of brave children from America, come all the way to Svalbard to ask a question: Might we, someday, need these seeds?"

"YES!"

"The Earth gives us food. The seeds give us a future. These children are here to protect it. America, you must pass their Planet Amendment so that we never have to open this vault."

Three more kids walk up to us, and as they get closer, we recognize them. One has blond hair in fringes over her forehead and blue eyes that look like sea glass.

"That's Melina," Jaesang says. "Her grandfather is the governor of West Virginia."

Another is a sixteen-year-old boy, and if he stood with his back against our Wall of Heights at home, he'd be halfway between me and Yao Ming.

"That's Evan," Catalina says, "the grandson of the Wyoming governor."

"And that's Jimmy," Alistair says, "the grandson of the Montana governor, with his mom."

When they heard that some planet activists had occupied Svalbard, they wanted to be a part of it, so they chartered a plane to Longyearbyen.

They hold up an American flag with the single word in all caps: RATIFY. Catalina and Zoe exchange a look. They step away.

Melina from West Virginia takes the bullhorn from Greta.

"Hello, World. My name is Melina Law. I come from West Virginia, a beautiful state in America, famous for the Blue Ridge Mountains. I love my grandpa, Governor Jim Law. He taught me that you have to have courage to make change. He used to coach basketball, and he always told us that if you throw the ball east and west, you best make sure that the pass is caught. But if you throw it away down the court, that's fine. At least you were trying

188
★

to get something done. To my grandpa in the Governor's Mansion, I say, we've been tossing the ball east and west on climate change for too long. Pretty soon, Grandpa, this'll be a buzzer shot. And if we don't make it, it won't be just one season lost, but all of them till kingdom come."

And then more and more people march up the hill to help us occupy the seed vault. Hundreds, maybe a thousand, protestors. They take up our chants:

"WHAT DO WE WANT? CLIMATE JUSTICE. WHEN DO WE WANT IT? NOW!"

And "THERE'S NO PLAN B FOR THE PLANET."

And "RATIFY! RATIFY! RATIFY!"

As if on cue, an enormous banner unrolls from the top of the seed vault's glass wall. Six bedsheets stitched together, each with one bold letter to spell one big word:

R-A-T-I-F-Y

At the top of the glass wall, Catalina and Zoe stand with their feet on the banner and their fists to the sky.

The crowd whoops and howls. We're making a lot of noise out here. It feels, for once, like our climate message is finally being heard.

We're so loud you *almost* can't hear the helicopter that swoops down and lands in front of us. Soldiers from the Norwegian Home Guard spill out and give us orders to stand down.

We have no choice but to surrender. They put us in zip ties and march us toward the whirling blade.

"Wait," Melina says. "Arrest me too."

20

The Norwegian Prison System

"I liked your speech," I shout to Melina.

We're in a Norwegian Home Guard helicopter, being transported to the mainland.

"Thanks," she says. "What's your name?"

"Sam."

"Melina."

We can't shake hands—they're in zip ties—so we just smile. I feel a little woozy in the stomach. Must be the flight.

"So what do you like to do when you're not kidnapping seeds?" she shouts.

"Me? I like to play music. Mostly jazz."

"Ever listen to bluegrass?"

I shake my head no. She gives the Norwegian soldier a look. He pulls out one of her AirPods and puts it in my ear. I hear a banjo and an accent, but I can't make out the words. Still, my foot starts tapping the floor.

"What do you like to do when you're not listening to blue-grass?" I ask.

"I train dogs. I take them to competitions."

She tells me about the different breeds she's trained, blood-hounds and beagles and terriers. She tells me that her favorite book is *Where the Red Fern Grows*.

When we land on the prison yard in Tromsø, Norway, I hear Catalina say to Zoe, "You like dogs?"

And Zoe says, "Used to."

The guardsman escorts us off the helicopter toward the prison doors. Alistair tells us not to worry. It's got 4.7 stars on Tripadvisor.

"Seriously? Who rates a prison?"

"Some guy was here for nine months and six days. Said conditions are good. Small room, but decent food and kind staff. Much better than in Russia."

"I wonder what he was in for," Jaesang says.

After we get "processed"—fingerprinted, photographed, and interrogated—we're taken by van to the Nord-Troms District courthouse, where, unfortunately, we meet a man from the Regjeringsadvokatembetet—don't ask me how to pronounce that. The regjeringsadvokat—attorney for the king—is the Norwegian equivalent of the U.S. attorney general. And this one has an extreme dislike of scofflaws and student activists.

He charges us with grand theft radio, intimidation of a government employee, impersonating a school official, and 500,000,000 counts of seednapping. One for each seed. The maximum sentence for our crimes: 230 years.

Fortunately, Mr. Kalman, who had complained of chest pains and been medevaced to Tromsø ER, was feeling much better and Ubered straight to the courthouse.

Through a translator, Mr. Kalman asks Justice Unni Aksel to dismiss the charges. "They're minors. And it's a first offense."

"Not for all of them," the regjeringsadvokat says, glaring at Alistair. "One was arrested for disruption of interstate commerce in America."

"A first offense on Norwegian soil," Mr. Kalman corrects.

The justice agrees to let us out. "*After* you reimburse the Norwegian government for expenses related to your clients' publicity stunt."

She pulls out an old-fashioned adding machine, with a roll of paper that you tear off when you get a total, and does a series of calculations. With each subtotal her red lips part, her brown eyebrows jump up, her green eyes pop.

Finally, she presses the star key on her adding machine, which not only gives the total but advances the tape. She tears it off and sets our fine at . . .

"Seven hundred and fifty thousand kroner. Each."

"That's ninety thousand dollars!" Catalina says.

"It would take me a year to earn that!" Alistair says.

"You must have a good job," Justice Aksel says. And her gavel comes down.

• • •

We spend the night in tiny cells in Tromsø Prison. Me and Alistair bunk together. He tells me he's going to give the place two stars.

"They should've had a vegetarian option at dinner."

We each get one phone call or FaceTime. Jaesang FaceTimes his grandpa. He tells him all about the storm and the ice fjords, and he says he hopes he can bring him here someday before all the ice is gone.

Alistair is on his iPad, FaceTiming home.

"Can I talk to James?"

The camera turns away from his parents and makes the wobbly walk outside . . . and down low to the ground. There, in his rosemary burrow, is Alistair's tortoise, James.

"Hi'ya, Buddy. It's me, Alistair. A long way from home. You wouldn't like it here, James. Too cold for a tortoise. But I'm not scared. We're doing the right thing, fighting for the planet. For you. If they slap multiple life sentences on me, there's a chance you won't live to see me released. I just want to say I love you, Jimmy. You're the best tortoise a boy could ever have."

He starts to cry, then hands me the iPad. "Take it, Sam. I don't want him to worry."

Catalina is on the phone to her grandma. "Sí, Abuela. Mi siento fuerte."

I glance over at Zoe, who's not on any phone, and I realize that all her people are here.

Which makes me miss my mom.

"Sam," she says when our FaceTime connects. "Are you okay? Are you afraid?"

"I'm not afraid, Mom. I'm disappointed. We came this far to get the world's attention, and it might've all been for nothing."

"Nothing? You're all over the internet. You made CNN, NPR, MSNBC, and *Fox News*. You're on the cover of the *New York Times*."

She holds the newspaper up to the camera. There's a picture of us with Greta and a crowd of kids in front of the seed vault, Zoe and Catalina's banner above our heads.

"Have they voted in Montana yet? Have they voted in West Virginia?"

"Montana was a yes. And Kansas voted yes."

"What about Iowa?"

"Iowa hasn't voted. Neither have Wyoming and West Virginia."

"So we still have a chance?"

195
★

"Yes, Sam. You still have a chance. But when are they letting you out of jail?"

"Oh, just as soon as we come up with ninety thousand dollars times five kids. That's four hundred and sixty thousand."

"Four hundred fifty thousand," Catalina says from her cell.

"What if you can't raise that kind of money?"

"Alistair might have to have his bar mitzvah in prison. And Catalina her quinceañera. And Jaesang his Coming-of-Age Day. And me my twenty-first birthday."

"Honey, I'm sure Mr. Kalman will think of something."

"He's clever, Mom. Not rich. We spent our climate budget on ads."

• • •

Later that night, the guard tells us we have a visitor. The iron doors at the end of the hall clang open, and in walks Mr. Kalman. "Gather around, kids," he says. "I've got something to say."

We can't exactly gather around, but we all come to the front of our cells, lean our foreheads against the bars, and look at him.

"I wasn't much older than you the first time I got thrown in jail. It was in Jackson, Mississippi. I had joined up with a group called the Freedom Riders. We were protesters, Black and white, who wanted to end segregation on buses in the South. We rode the buses together, side by side, in violation of the law. The minute we stepped off that bus, we got arrested and thrown into Parchman State Penitentiary."

"Were you afraid, Mr. Kalman?"

"Yes, Catalina, I was. They did some terrible things to us in that prison. But we banded together because we knew what we'd done was right. And when we finally got out, we stepped into a changed world. I believe the world is changing now, too. In no small part because of what you've done here."

He pulls a folded paper from his pocket, unfolds it, and holds up a smaller version of our map: the Road to Ratification.

We stand there, shocked. In a good way.

Iowa is green. So is Missouri. We got Indiana and Ohio too. If we could just get three more . . .

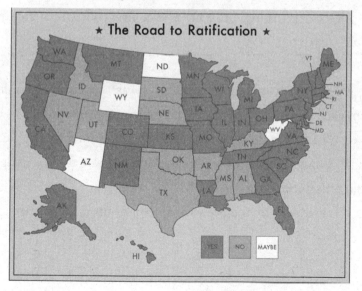

• • •

The next morning when we wake up, the guard tells us we're free.

"Free? How? Why?"

"Your fine has been paid."

In the bright morning light, I'm expecting to see Melina's grandpa. Not only is he the governor of West Virginia, but at dinner last night she told us how he inherited a coal mining business from his dad and then started a bunch of other companies. He's worth more than a billion dollars.

But it's not billionaire Jim Law who bailed us out of Norwegian jail.

It's not even a grownup.

"Greta?" Alistair says as soon as our eyes adjust to the light.

"Good morning, Alistair. Hello, everyone. You are free now."

"How?"

"I have ten million followers on Instagram., and I asked them each to send ten cents. Seven million contributed."

"What'd you do with the extra two hundred and fifty thousand?" Catalina asks while I'm looking around for the judge's adding machine.

"I divided it by the number of contributors. Each got a refund of —"

"Three and a half cents," she and Catalina say.

"How can we ever thank you?" Zoe asks.

She looks at Alistair. "One of you offered to make me dinner."

21

Alistair Cooks

When Captain Knudsen heard they took us to Tromsø, he set sail for the port and is now offering us a ride to America. The *Roald Amundsen* hasn't had this many passengers since it was a fully operational cruise ship. Our team is back together but bigger now. Grandchildren of governors have come aboard. Justice Aksel is taking her first holiday in three years to sail with us. Astrid has left her post at the seed vault because, she said, she wanted to be part of history.

Evan from Wyoming told his grandpa he'd be sailing home to the United States. The governor told him to get on the next plane NOW.

"Sorry, Grandpa," the boy said. "I've been flygskammed —as they say in Swedish—into traveling more sustainably from now on."

The governor of Wyoming hung up on his grandson.

Captain Knudsen charts our course from the Norwegian

Sea into the North Sea, across the English Channel, and down through the North Atlantic to New York, with a brief stop in Gothenburg to drop off Greta. We'll be a total of seven days at sea.

Alistair spends much of the first day in the galley. While we're looking through the Blue Eye at the impossibly beautiful world below water and, through our own eyes, at the icy landscape above, he's busy cooking.

"Dinner at five," he says.

Even though we have all kinds of distractions — the scenery, Ping-Pong, the track and basketball courts on A deck, and all those science toys, we can't keep our minds off the one fact that hangs over this day: it's exactly five months since Mr. Becerra transmitted our Planet Amendment to the fifty United States for their vote. We've gotten thirty-five states to ratify. If we don't win three of the last four states — North Dakota, Wyoming, Arizona, and West Virginia — ours will be the seventh amendment in U.S. history that passed Congress but died in the states.

"I just realized," Catalina says. "Here we are on the last day, and we need three-quarters of the remaining states to ratify. That's the same ratio of the total number of states that the Constitution says we need."

Catalina and math!

It's not looking good. Evan just came to say "The Wyoming Legislature voted against the Planet Amendment."

He tells us that they stayed through the night for debate, and the vote came at seven a.m. Mountain Time.

Catalina unrolls our master tally. She colors Wyoming red and updates the total: 35 yes, 12 no.

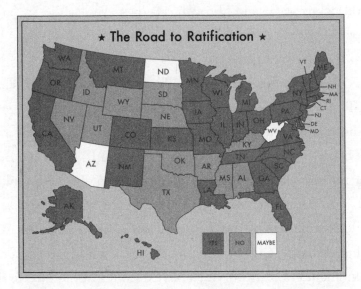

"With thirty-five yeses," Jaesang says, "you'd think we already won."

It isn't easy to get to thirty-eight. Especially when you have to make it past conservative Arizona and coal-rich West Virginia.

• • •

At 3:30 Jaesang screen mirrors from his laptop to the video wall, where CNN'S breaking news banner reads PLANET AMENDMENT'S LAST GASP.

The commentators are comparing our cause to a fish on deck gasping for air.

"More like a polar bear desperately searching for ice," Zoe says.

I feel like we should have stayed in Svalbard. Like maybe we surrendered too easily. But Catalina reminds me that we're just kids, after all. "Not soldiers with guns."

"You have something more powerful than guns," a quiet voice says. "You have truth."

We turn and see Greta standing off to the side, looking out the tall window at the sea. There's something about her that makes me want to slow down and listen, and look, and think. I've had this feeling before, when we were inside the Supreme Court, and when we saw the polar bear on Svalbard. I've felt it under the Capitol dome and under our magnolia tree at school.

"I schoolstriked for the planet," she says. "It was a first step. Many things have changed since then. Not enough, but it was a beginning. Then you wrote an amendment to your Constitution. It may not pass today, but it is a big step. There will have to be more. At least we are moving—what did your grandfather say, Melina—*down the court?*"

"Yeah. We keep passing down the court."

The breaking news banner flashes a sign of hope. North Dakota just voted yes.

They cut to John King at the Magic Wall. "I'm getting fresh information now from our correspondent in North Dakota, where they've just voted to ratify the Planet Amendment. That's thirty-six yeses to twelve nos. Still waiting on Arizona and West Virginia. I have to say, Wolf, it doesn't look good for these young climate warriors."

It gets very quiet on the *Roald Amundsen*. So quiet that you can hear the clatter of pots and pans in the galley, the clop of a knife chopping, and the sizzle of something hitting a hot pan.

But the sounds from the kitchen get swallowed by a cheer when Arizona lights up green. The Grand Canyon State just said *yes!*

"I guess they're banking on a solar-powered future," Wolf Blitzer says on-screen.

Melina's cell phone dings: a text from her grandpa. She reads it aloud: "*Going into a press conference. Hope you'll understand.*"

Melina's grandpa, Governor Jim Law, is famous for his press conferences. People tune in on YouTube just to watch this old-timer talk. He's a big man, too. A gentle giant, they call him.

Jaesang pulls up the press conference on YouTube. Governor Law, Grandpa Law, fills the screen.

"Good morning, everyone. I've called this press conference to talk about two things: the climate and the economy. What I want to say is simply this: they're two legs, and if you cut one, the other can't stand. I just spoke with my friend Mitch Gardner of Wyoming. He told me that his great state said no to the Planet Amendment now pending in the legislatures. Jim, he said, Wyoming will not stand idly by and let anyone else write our next chapter. He urged me to recommend a no vote too.

"With Wyoming's no, and the yes votes from Arizona and North Dakota, our little state of West Virginia now holds the deciding vote. That's an awesome responsibility for the Mountain State.

"The economy and the climate. Two legs on which we all stand. My daddy used to tell me, Son, he'd say, stick your hand in a bucket of water and don't move it. Then jerk it out of the water real quick and watch the water. It'll be turbulent for a while. But just stand there watching, and the water'll settle down.

"Now, as governor of our great state, I don't have a say in the ratification or rejection of this amendment. It's a parliamentary matter, not my place to sway the vote. But I do have the power to convene a special joint session of the legislature, which I have done. I will be heading over to the capitol now to be there. Whichever way it goes, I want you to know simply this: stand there watching. Eventually the water will settle down."

"I don't get it," Jaesang says.

"Me either," Catalina says. "What does a bucket of water have to do with climate change?"

"It's polluted," I say.

"It's a metaphor," Melina says. "My grandpa always talks in metaphors. What he means is no matter how the vote goes, one side or the other is going to be real ornery at the result. But in time, people will move on."

"We don't have time to move on from climate change," I say.

"I know that, Sam. You know that. Kids everywhere know it. But the world's full of grownups who don't."

She watches the screen as her grandpa, Governor Law, walks out of the room.

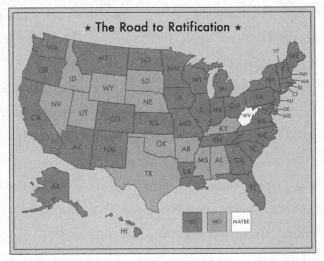

• • •

It's 4:30 on our ship's clock—10:30 in West Virginia—when the in-person vote begins in the joint session of the West Virginia Senate and its House of Delegates. The clerk of the legislature addresses the room.

"Good morning, Senators and Delegates to the House. The governor called this joint session for a vote on the proposed Twenty-Eighth Amendment to the United States Constitution, known as the Planet Amendment. In order to ratify here, the amendment needs to win a simple majority in both houses. I will call the names of our thirty-four senators and one hundred delegates to the house. We begin with the senators. Mr. Andervelt."

"Nay."

"Mr. Andervelt votes nay. Mr. Barton."

"Aye."

"Mr. Barton votes aye. Mr. Bork . . ."

She goes down the roster of thirty-four senators . . . and as we sit and keep the tally, I begin to smell something rich and woodsy coming from the ship's galley. It smells like Thanksgiving without the turkey, but then I hear a *ding* and a moment later recognize the scent of chocolate, and I remember something Alistair once told me about how he cooks.

"I work backwards, Sam. From dessert to appetizers."

He must have put his vegan chocolate soufflé in the oven,

then made his mushroom meatballs, and now he's probably working on the vegetarian smorgasbord.

"Mr. Unterseyer."

"Aye."

"Mr. Unterseyer votes aye. Mr. Witherspoon."

"Nay."

"Mr. Witherspoon votes nay."

Now we're getting so hungry I can hear stomachs rumbling in the room. It's almost eleven a.m. in West Virginia, five o'clock here on the Norwegian Sea, and Alistair promised us a sit-down dinner in Greta's honor at five.

He's one minute late.

The final tally in the West Virginia senate: 17 to 17, so we're tied.

Captain Knudsen comes out of the galley wearing an apron. He rings a cowbell for attention.

"Chefmaster Alistair would like you to come to table now."

Two minutes late. Pretty good, Alistair, in a foreign kitchen far from home.

Meanwhile, on the big screen, we watch the tally continue in the West Virginia House of Delegates.

"Mr. Albertson."

"Nay."

"Mr. Albertson votes nay. Mr. Diller."

"Aye."

"Mr. Diller votes aye. Ms. Everett."

"Nay."

"Ms. Everett votes nay."

The screen is split: CNN's live coverage of the vote on one side, the grand tally on the other. We're tied in the senate, trailing in the house, 32 to 28, with forty votes left.

The passengers on the *Roald Amundsen* take seats in the dining room. We do that automatic thing of grownups at one table, kids at another. Melina grabs a seat with Catalina, Zoe, Jaesang, and me.

Mr. Kalman, Betty, Astrid, and Justice Aksel sit at the grownups' table. I glance over and see Greta standing by the window, looking out at a tiny island of floating ice. It looks like a missing piece from one of the larger icebergs nearby.

I call over to her.

"Greta, want to sit with us?"

"Ms. Fogerty."

"Aye."

"Ms. Fogerty votes aye."

I see her eyes go from the crowded kids' table to the roomier grownups' table. And I remember that quote from her mom's book about her. *"Friends are children and all children are mean."*

"We can squeeze in," I say.

She looks at me, looks at the table full of kids, and smiles.

"Mr. Hagelbottom."

"Nay."

"Mr. Hagelbottom votes nay. Mr. Hobbes."

"Aye."

We make room for Greta. I can't imagine kids anywhere, ever, being mean to her. After Alistair finished reading the book about her, he told us that she has Asperger's syndrome. She sees what a lot of people let themselves ignore, and she's not afraid to call them out on it. Greta said that her Asperger's is a superpower. Who wouldn't want a superhero at their table?

"What do you think Alistair has prepared for us?" she asks.

"With Alistair," I say, "you never know."

The door to the galley swings open, and out comes Captain Knudsen carrying a huge platter of pickled everything—carrots, red and orange peppers, beets, olives, green beans. Crispy flatbread on the side. Four different cheeses.

"Chefmaster Alistair would like me to convey to the table that this evening's entire smorgasbord is vegan. Including the cheeses."

Greta smiles. We pass around the platter and fill our plates.

I glance at the video wall: 34 nays, 30 ayes. We still don't know if this meal will be a celebration or a consolation prize. But we're down by four, and West Virginia is a conservative state. If the vote goes along party lines, Alistair's feast will taste like failure. I think about the woman I met who was scared of losing her job if the meat processing plant closed. Would she vote no? Or would she feel maybe it's time for a new job that's good for the people and the planet?

But what if that job doesn't exist yet?

"Mr. Platt votes nay. Mr. Poynter?"

"Aye."

"Mr. Poynter votes aye."

Alistair's smorgasbord looks so good, smells so good, *is* so good . . . but after one or two bites, Catalina says, "I'm too nervous to eat."

"Me too," Jaesang says.

"Me too," Zoe says.

"Me too," I say.

Over at the grownups' table, they're drinking Norwegian beer and chowing down.

"Mr. Kalman, how can you eat at a time like this?"

"Sam," he says, "at a time like this, how can you not?"

It must be a generational thing. Ours is more terrified of the future.

"Mr. Putter votes aye. Mr. Quentin?"

"Aye."

"Mr. Quentin votes aye."

I can't help it. That's two ayes in a row. To celebrate, I take a nibble of nut cheese. Better than I was expecting.

"Mr. Reddenbacker?"

"Nay."

"Mr. Reddenbacker votes nay."

Jaesang updates the total: 44 nays, 43 ayes. We're down by one with thirteen delegates to go. I jump up from the table and run into the galley.

"No passengers allowed in the galley!" Alistair barks.

"It's getting close. You should come watch."

He nods, adjusts the heat on a simmering pot of thick tomato sauce, and wipes his hands on his apron. He turns to the captain. "Six more minutes on the sauce. Don't touch the heat." He follows me into the dining room . . .

. . . where the total is now 47 to 44. Down by three.

"Ms. Wilkins?"

"Aye."

"Ms. Wilkins votes aye. Mr. Wogensen?"

"Nay."

"Mr. Wogensen votes nay."

48 to 45.

"Mr. Bernard Yates?"

"Nay."

"Mr. Bernard Yates votes nay. Mr. Gerald Yates?"

"Aye."

"Mr. Gerald Yates votes aye."

It's 49 to 46. Just five votes to go. If we catch them, it'll be a miracle. But like Governor Law said, we've got to keep throwing the ball down the court.

The ship is dead quiet. The grownups aren't even noshing.

"Mr. Youkeles?"

"Aye."

"Mr. Youkeles votes aye."

49 to 47.

"Mr. Yule?"

We see a broad-shouldered man with a thick but well-trimmed beard approach the podium. He's the assistant majority whip and the vice chair of the Homeland Security Committee. He's on Agricultural and Natural Resources, but he's also on Banking and Insurance. Could go either way.

His bio lists five kids. A good sign . . .

"Aye."

"Mr. Yule votes aye."

49 to 48. We need at least two more votes to keep our hopes alive. The planet needs them. Just. Two. More. Votes.

"Ms. Zayle?"

"Cora Zayle," Zoe reports. "She's on two committees: Natural Resources, a plus, but also Energy and Manufacturing."

"Anything in the bio?"

"Bio's blank. Just a picture."

We look at her picture. She seems young, but we can't tell if she's climate-friendly. Until she says, "Aye."

Tied at 49!

"Ms. Zayle votes aye. Mr. Zucker?"

Jaesang is ready with his stats. "Workforce Development. Also on Energy and Manufacturing. No mention of any kids."

On-screen, we see an older gentleman in a brown suit, white shirt, and yellow and blue polka-dot tie step up to the lectern. He has gray hair and a kind face. He reminds me of Mr. Kalman.

Except in the way he votes.

"Nay."

"Mr. Zucker votes nay."

50 to 49. It's going to be a buzzer shot.

There's only one delegate left. Catalina already clicked on her profile. "Liza Zukmann. She sits on the Seniors, Children and Family Issues Committee. That's promising."

"Bio?"

"Born 1962. B.A. poly sci from West Virginia University. Married with two kids. Member of the Marshall County Animal Rescue . . . Open Arms Ladies Bible Study."

Animal rescue . . . Bible study . . . Two kids? She's gotta vote aye.

The clerk calls her name.

"Ms. Zukmann?"

Aw, Snap.

That's what shows up on the video wall. Along with a message: *Please check your internet connection.*

22

Dinner Is Served

I saw *Titanic*. I know things can go horribly wrong in cold seas.

"Did we hit an iceberg?" I ask.

"Must have come into a dead zone between mountains," the captain says. "Sorry, kids—sometimes the *Roald Amundsen* loses internet."

"Can you radio the coast guard?"

"Only for emergencies. We have to keep that channel open. I'm afraid you'll have to wait until we're in port in Gothenburg."

"How long?"

"An hour."

"Well, then," Alistair says, "we'd better eat."

• • •

Alistair's smorgasbord was delicious, but what floats out of his kitchen next, on a platter held by the captain's hands, is dazzling —a steaming hot, rich, creamy confection of Swedish Earthballs next to a cloud of buttery mashed potatoes. Nearby, a circle of roasted carrots, green beans, and parsnips. I smell tarragon and caramelized onions, butter and cream, salt air from the sea, and sweet air from his kitchen.

The captain dips the platter toward Greta as if it's his dance partner.

Greta inhales . . . Greta sighs . . . and Greta starts to cry. Yep, she and Alistair have something else in common. Tears.

"I haven't smelled this blend of nutmeg, allspice, onion, and meat since I was a little girl. My mother would make them for me with" — she cries some more — "mashed potatoes. How did you know?"

"I cheated," Alistair says. "I read her book about you. And there's no meat. The sauce comes from *Recipes of Sweden: A Classic Swedish Cookbook* by Inga Norberg. But I used my own mushroom-almond paté to make Swedish Earthballs à la Greta."

"Oh, Alistair, it's wonderful."

"You haven't tasted it yet."

He spoons some mashed potatoes and Earthballs onto her plate and adds roasted vegetables, making sure to scoop up some of the buttery sauce and drizzle it on top.

She looks at the chef, looks at the food, and takes a bite.

A soft sound, something between a grunt and a sigh, comes from her throat. But the rest of her . . . total poker face. No words, either. She takes another bite, this time lifting a dollop of mashed potatoes along with the hearty tomato sauce and part of an Earthball. Her eyes go wide. Her grunt gets louder.

Still no words.

"The mashed potatoes," Alistair says, "are Mr. Kalman's recipe. He uses a secret ingredient. I can't tell you what it is. Okay, I can't *not* tell. A pinch of sugar. Actually, more than a pinch."

Her fork returns to the plate, this time capturing it all—the meatless meatballs, the mashed potatoes, the gravy, even a sprig of parsley—all in one bite.

"Oh, Alistair," she says, finally looking up at him, "I wish you could cook for me for the rest of my life."

"I can," he says. "And for way less than seven hundred and fifty thousand Norwegian kroner a year."

We still don't know if we got the last vote. But we're sailing toward Sweden, eating Alistair's perfect food, here with friends. If we have to go on fighting, we will. For now, though, for an hour more, life is good.

23

We Finally Get Wi-Fi

The **Roald Amundsen** **glides** into Skagerrak Fjord between Denmark and Norway, and as we round Skagen, at the top of Denmark just across from Gothenburg, the ship's dining hall sounds like someone is banging a giant xylophone. *Ping, ping, ping-ping. Ping.* It's our cell phones getting a flood of texts.

The CNN signal is back on the video wall:

BREAKING NEWS

50–50

"It's a tie in West Virginia," Catalina says.

"If it's a tie, it's not a majority," Jaesang says. "We lose."

"Every state makes its own rules," Catalina says. "We don't know what happens in West Virginia."

We all turn to Melina.

"How should I know?" she says.

"Your grandpa's the governor!"

"But I haven't read the state constitution."

On the video wall we see CNN go to a commercial break. Jaesang has already found a PDF of the West Virginia State Constitution on his phone and is speed-reading for "legislative procedures."

"It says '*no citizen shall fight a duel with deadly weapons.*' Sorry, wrong section . . . Here it is, and I quote. '*In the event of a deadlocked, or tie vote, in both the House of Delegates and the Senate with respect to a proposed Amendment to the state or federal Constitution, the governor shall cast the deciding vote.*'"

We hear one more *ding* on somebody's cell phone. We all look at ours, but it's Melina who says, "It's from my grandpa. *A good governor has to put the people first.*"

The *people* first, I worry. Not the planet.

Suddenly a name pops into my head. "Harry T. Burn!" I say, and everyone looks at me.

Betty knows who he is. So does Mr. Kalman. He looks at me and nods. "Harry T. Burn."

"Who's Harry T. Burn?" Melina asks.

"Harry T. Burn," I tell her, "was the young state representative from Tennessee who cast the deciding vote for the Nineteenth Amendment. It gave women the right to vote."

"What does that have to do with my grandpa?"

"Harry T. Burn was going to vote no when he received a letter from his mom at the last minute. She told him to do the right thing."

"I get it. You want me to text my grandpa. Tell *him* to do the right thing."

We all nod.

"And tell him you love him," I say.

Melina picks up her phone.

Back from commercial, CNN broadcasts from the floor of the West Virginia House of Delegates. We see Governor Law enter the room, shake a few hands, and make his way to the lectern. An aide lifts the microphone to the governor's towering height.

"Lord a livin', this is one close vote. I have been asked by the speaker of the house to come over here and fulfill a constitutional duty as your governor. Now, in some states, a tie in a legislative matter is just that. A tie. It fails to receive a simple majority of votes, and it doesn't pass. But in a matter as consequential as amending the United States Constitution, our little state of West Virginia sees things differently. In a deadlock, we ask the governor to cast the deciding vote. That puts the future of the nation's economy and the world's environment on the shoulders of one person. Me."

Just then the microphone picks up a *buzz-buzz* from his cell phone. On the TV, we see him glance down at his phone.

"He's reading my text," Melina says.

But he's not reacting to it, except to pause and think. Then he puts his phone in his pocket, pulls the microphone close to his mouth, and speaks.

"Now, I know this: I'm going to upset some dear friends and maybe some dear family members too with my vote. But I have always put the people of West Virginia first in my heart and front in my mind. And that's where they sit now as I contemplate this proposed amendment to the Constitution of our great country.

"'*A stable climate being necessary for the survival of life on Earth, the right of the people to inhabit a planet free from pollution and unnatural warming shall not be infringed.*'

"Well, at what cost? Jobs? Surely. A significant loss of jobs in this coal-rich state and others. Revenue? A lot of lost revenue, to be sure. Pain? In the near term, yes, a lot of pain.

"What about the long term? I believe that here in West Virginia we have a natural resource richer than coal and gas. You don't have to blow off a mountain top or drill into the ground to tap it. It's a resource that dreams up big ideas, big change. And it's right there in the minds of children in the Mountain State and beyond. Children wrote this amendment. Children foresee what we adults have allowed ourselves to ignore. It comes from the Bible, from the Book of Isaiah: 'The wolf shall dwell with the lamb, and the leopard shall lie down with the young goat, and the calf and the lion and the fattened calf together; and a little child shall lead them.' Climate change is a beast that only children, it seems, can tame.

"Those who know me know I used to coach baseball too. We have an expression on the diamond. We say, tie goes to the runner."

"I don't get it," Alistair says.

"Just watch," Melina says.

"Governor Law, in the business before our legislature this day, whether the state of West Virginia shall ratify the proposed Twenty-Eighth Amendment to the United States Constitution, how do you cast your vote?"

"I cast my vote . . . aye."

"The governor votes aye. The amendment is ratified."

The amendment is ratified! We leap so high that when we land, the *Roald Amundsen* rocks.

Know who else rocks? Governor Jim Law of West Virginia.

"Tie goes to the runner. I still don't get it," Alistair says. "I'm better with cooking metaphors."

"Alistair," I say, "the runner is the one going somewhere, trying to get something bold to happen. Like steal a base. Or save the planet."

"Alistair," Greta says, "*you're* the runner."

"I am?"

"Because of you, we're all headed into a clean, green future."

Alistair looks at her. He looks at me and Jae and Zoe and Cat, at Mr. Kalman and Betty and Melina and the captain and his first officer and Astrid and Justice Askel—basically, everyone who got us here.

"No," he says. "We're all the runner."

He raises his glass of virgin gløgg.

"Skål!"

"Skål!" we all shout.

And Catalina makes one last mark on our map.

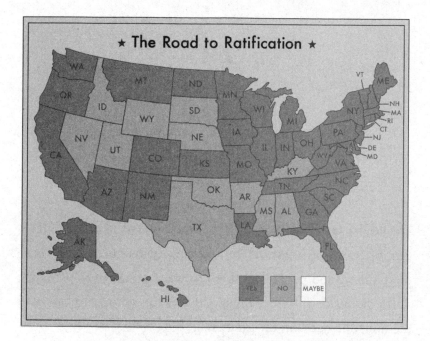

★ The Road to Ratification ★

YES   NO   MAYBE

24

Home

We're in Gothenburg just long enough to refuel and return Greta to her home. As the *Amundsen* drifts out of port, more than a thousand people are there to wave goodbye to us. Greta walks alongside the ship, smiling at Alistair, who leans out over the hull, one hand on the safety rail.

"Don't fall, Alistair."

"Too late. I already have."

"I'm too old for you."

"In ten years, I'll be twenty-two. You'll only be twenty-eight."

"Yes, but in fifty more years I'll be seventy-eight, and you will still be young. Seventy-two."

"Exactly. You'll need a younger man to carry your duffel for you. To cook for you. Think about it, Greta. Food in a retirement home. Or fresh-made meals from Chefmaster Alistair."

"Fresh-made sounds better. Absolutt! But for now, skriv till mig."

"Jag lovar. But, Greta, STOP!"

"Stop what?"

"Walking. NOW!"

She's almost at the edge of the quay. She catches herself just in time, laughs, and waves us off.

As we sail back through Skagerrak Fjord, Mr. Kalman asks the captain if he can chart a new destination.

"Where to?"

"Washington, D.C. The presence of these climate warriors has been requested at the National Archives."

Six more days at sea. At least there's a Ping-Pong table.

• • •

"Sam, want to play?"

"Sure, Catalina."

"Oh. I was going to ask him," Zoe says.

"Me too," Melina says.

I look at the three girls.

"Uh, actually I'm in the mood for a sauna."

It's just me and Mr. Kalman in the shvitz house, as he calls the sauna. We sit side by side on the hot wooden bench. Out the glass window there's a view of B deck, where the sun is bright and Betty is lying on a chaise, reading a book. Jaesang, Alistair, and Captain Knudsen are sharing a pair of binoculars, gazing at birds. To the right, I see Catalina, Zoe, and Melina playing King at the Ping-Pong table. Straight ahead, the vast North Atlantic Sea.

"I need some advice, Mr. Kalman."

"I've got a lot to give, Sam."

"Okay, say you're a guy and you like a girl."

"Yeah?"

"But you also like another girl."

"You wouldn't be the first."

"But you like a *third* girl too."

"Now you're veering toward trouble."

"That's why I need advice. I always liked Catalina. And then I met Zoe and I liked her too. And then I met Melina and had this weird feeling in my stomach, like I was seasick even though we were in a helicopter."

"That's airsickness."

"I still felt it on the ground."

"That's a crush."

"But I feel it around Zoe and Catalina too."

"That's a triple crush."

"What do I do?"

"In my experience, friendship with two girls will outlast a romance with one."

"How about a romance with three?"

"That'll be over before you know it. I say, be friends with

228
★

them all. Give it some time. Your heart will tell you the right thing to do."

He leans his head back against the warm wood. I keep looking out the window. Especially the right side.

"What about you, Mr. Kalman?"

"Well, Betty and I are getting married Thursday on the steps of the U.S. Supreme Court."

"What???? I thought you two couldn't stand each other."

"Appearances are often deceptive, Sam. Bickering like ours can belie a well-concealed mutual regard."

"But shouldn't you, I don't know, date awhile first?"

He turns to me, smiles, shakes his head. "A new companion is a blessing at any age. At ours, it's a miracle."

• • •

On the Thursday morning after the Wednesday after the Tuesday a week later—at least I think it's a Thursday—when you've spent so much time at sea, every day is Blursday—we dock at the Port of Washington, D.C. Our legs feel like rubber as we head up the gangway onto firm ground. But if there's one thing that can get your land legs back, it's the stone steps of the National Archives, which we climb at ten a.m. for our appointment with the archivist.

"Back so soon?" Mr. Becerra says when we come through the security check. "Seems like just yesterday that you were here."

But more than 150 days have passed. One hundred fifty days that, just maybe, saved the world.

"I wanted you to be the first, other than me and the printer, of course—to see your amendment in print. Copies will be sent to both houses of Congress at noon. And there will be a little ceremony at three in the White House Rose Garden. The president, as you know, has put climate change high on his list of priorities."

"What if he gets kicked out in the next election?" Alistair says. "What if the next president goes back to polluting?"

"Then he or she violates their oath of office to uphold the Constitution, Alistair. A Constitution that now protects the planet, thanks to you."

He unrolls a scroll of the updated U.S. Constitution. At the very top, in big font, it says WE THE PEOPLE. At the very bottom, these new words:

Amendment XXVIII. A stable climate being necessary for the survival of life on Earth, the right of the people to inhabit a planet free from pollution and unnatural warming shall not be infringed.

We just stand there, pretty much awestruck, at the sight of those words that we wrote, now officially part of history.

I keep thinking about how strange it is that humans are the only living things that make trash. The only ones that actually upset the balance of nature by the way we live. We're also the only species that can solve this huge mess of our own making. Jaesang reads up on these things, and he was telling me about some of the crazy ideas climate scientists are dreaming up in order to turn things around. Like we might start spraying particles that reflect light into the atmosphere. They'll bounce sunlight back into space and help reverse global warming. Or we might invent fake clouds to bring more rain where there's long-term drought. Maybe Catalina's idea about turning trees into solar power plants isn't so harebrained after all. But you've got to wonder, what new problems will come from our solutions to old ones? Will fake rain be safe rain? Will we turn the blue sky white?

If I think about all this too much, my anxiety pinches me and says, *You're not through with me yet, Sam.* But then I picture the glass sculpture at the Svalbard Global Seed Vault, with *its* tiny particles that reflect light. *Perpetual Repercussion.* A warning, yeah. But also a glimmer of hope.

My phone dings with a text. It's from Sadie, ten words that I'll never, ever delete: *Proud of you, Lil Bro. Proud of all you've done.*

• • •

We go straight from the archives to the steps of the Supreme Court, where I realize how much things have changed in a year.

231
★

For Mr. Kalman and Betty, who are exchanging wedding vows right now in front of the chief justice—he paused a case to come outside and perform the ceremony. For Alistair, who seems more confident than he was, who's definitely taller than he was. Changes in Jaesang, too, who seems happier, like maybe he can worry a little less about the coming storms. And in Catalina, who can worry a little less about what might fall from the sky onto little kids' heads. And a big change coming for Zoe. This morning she told us she's going back to regular school this semester.

"I'll be starting eighth grade at Reed," she said.

"Sweet," I say. "We'll all be in the same class."

As for me, well, I made up my mind about my three crushes. I can't really date the granddaughter of the governor. She lives in West Virginia, and that's, like, twenty-five hundred miles away from North Hollywood and would take me two hundred and one hours on my bike. But we can write to each other, like Alistair and Greta will, and for now, I'm good with that. And I'm good with keeping two great friends in Zoe and Catalina.

It's almost three, and we're in the Rose Garden of the White House. I make my way past reporters, dignitaries, scientists, and diplomats to the front row reserved for us. Catalina and Zoe scooch apart. "Can I sit with you?" I say, squeezing in between them.

Jaesang and Alistair file in next to us. It's a beautiful

September day, and soon the president comes out and steps up to the lectern. "Good afternoon," he says. "Today we welcome heroes of the planet. A planet that's been sick for a long time but, thanks to these brave young activists, will now have a chance to heal."

He calls us up to the front. Cameras click. People clap. And then he does something that I just know will make Alistair cry.

He says our names, one at a time, looking at each one of us as he does.

"Sam, Catalina, Jaesang, Zoe, Alistair . . . thank you. Tha—"

But he gets interrupted by Alistair, who, you guessed it, just exploded in tears.

"You okay?" I say.

He nods. Then shakes his head. "The president just said our names, Sam. I can't help it. I'm emotional."

"All right, okay. Take a minute."

"Look at all these people. In the Rose Garden. For us."

He breaks down again. The president waits.

"We did it, Sam," Alistair blubbers.

I put my arms around him. He's heaving now. And drenching my shirt.

"Just breathe, Alistair."

He does and settles down. I turn to the president.

"Okay, Mr. President. I think he's ready."

"I'm not sure I am," the president says, wiping away a tear. "I've always been a crier too, Alistair."

They look at each other and laugh through their tears. They cry a little more. Laugh a lot more. And then the president speaks.

"Thank you, kids. From the bottom of my heart. From the soul of the nation. Thank you for what you've done for the world."

He hangs medals around our necks.

The people start to clap and cheer. The applause spreads to Alistair's mom and my mom and dad, to Betty and to Jaesang's parents and to Catalina's whole extended family, who have come all the way from California—by train—to witness this great day.

It spreads to strangers and senators, to representatives and governors, Democrats and Republicans.

I don't know how long it'll last, but for this one moment we're one nation, one people, one planet.

I look out at the crowd, and I have to say, it feels pretty good to be here, in our nation's capital, for the biggest change of all.

To the Constitution.

EPILOGUE

Okay, so it's kind of hypocritical, but when we get home, there's a place we want to go to shop.

Not swap.

Shop.

I meet up with Cat and Alistair and Jacsang one Saturday on the corner of Magnolia and Lankershim, and we catch the 94 bus east to Glendale. We get off at the Americana mall, walk through as fast as we can because that's not the kind of shopping we've come to do, and then follow our phones three more blocks along East Broadway.

To Ed's Pet Shop.

We walk in, and right away I can tell this isn't your typical pet store. Instead of bumping into a rack of squeak toys, leashes, and treats on your way in, you step into an aviary, and you want to shut the door quick because you're afraid a bird'll fly out. Until you realize the birds are all safe behind a mesh screen. And they're not in some dinky cage. These parakeets, cockatiels, and parrots are airborne all over the warehouse-high shop. Jaesang just stands there, his head back, grinning like a pelican.

Just past the aviary, at waist level, you walk by a long table with a terrarium where tortoises are taking a slow-motion stroll, and Alistair strolls alongside them, saying hi to all these relatives of his friend James.

You can hear the hum and gurgle of water pumps on the opposite side of the aisle. It sounds like the waiting room at the dentist, but here it's not just one or two goldfish in a tank with plastic toys, it's a whole underwater world, with coral and rocks and reeds that sway in the current. Like something the Blue Eye would have recorded once, and maybe will again.

Right now it's Catalina's eye peering into the aquarium at a slow-floating seahorse.

Which leaves me as the only one to answer the man in a Save the Lemur T-shirt who steps out from the back of the store and says, "How can I help you?"

He's a small man, a little shorter than I am, but with stocky arms, tan skin, and big hair puffing up from his head. He looks like a mix of all the animals in the store.

"Are you Ed?" I say.

"Yup."

"I'm Sam. And these are my friends Jaesang, Alistair, and Catalina."

"You kids looking for a pet?"

"As a matter of fact, we are. A lost one."

"What kind?"

"A panther chameleon. It was donated to your store about three years ago. A girl had to give him up."

Ed shakes his head, as if he's heard this before.

"Lotsa kids get pets. They think it's going to be easy raising a living thing. But it's a commitment they don't always keep up."

"That's not why, Mister. Zoe could take care of anything —anyone—and she would've kept Benny if her parents hadn't—well, never mind. It just wasn't allowed."

"Zoe?"

"That's the girl."

"Benny?"

"That's the chameleon."

"Big eyes, bunch of spots on the side, delicate hands?"

"That's her!"

"I was talkin' about the chameleon. Ambilobe panther. A real beauty."

"He still here?"

"Sold. Not too long ago."

"Wait, really? Who bought him?"

"Lotta people come in here. It was a couple, I think. While back. They were holding hands. I told 'em be sure to wash before they picked up the chameleon. It's the little details people don't think of. They bought a book, too, so I know they care."

We all look at each other, crushed.

"Got some baby salamanders for sale. Maybe your friend would like one of those?"

"No thanks, Mister. It was Benny we were hoping to find."

On the bus back, we're all real quiet. Quiet and a little sad. At least we tried.

● ● ●

Back in the neighborhood, we stop by the NoHo to say hi to Mr. Kalman. He buzzes us in, and we take the stairs up to the second floor. We go past the lounge, where Betty is sitting with her memoir group. The room looks big without us.

We head up to the third floor, to apartment 303, and knock on the door. It's ajar, and a voice tells us to come on in.

Mr. Kalman is squatting, his hands on one end of a long box. Zoe has her hand on the other end. I'm worried that he'll throw his back out.

"Mr. Kalman," I say, "what are you doing?"

"You're just in time. Zoe and I are about to hoist this thing onto the table. But it might cause me to slip a disk. Give us a hand?"

"I got this," Jaesang says. He walks over, lifts the long box like it's Cracker Jacks, lays it down on the glass table under the TV.

"What is this thing?" he asks. "It's heavy."

"Open it and see."

Zoe smiles, cuts the thick plastic band around the cardboard box. The flaps fall.

"A terrarium," she says. Then she steps to the kitchen, washes her hands, and brings over a shoebox.

She pulls off the lid, reaches in, and when her hand comes up, I see she's holding something green. It looks like a lizard, only larger, with big eyes, spots on the side, and delicate hands.

A panther chameleon.

"Guys, say hello to Benny. The newest resident of the NoHo Senior Arts Colony."

We don't say hello. We don't say anything. We just stand there, totally dumbfounded.

"Benny?"

"That's right."

"*The* Benny?"

"The one and only."

A nice couple who were holding hands. He forgot to mention that one was twelve and the other ninety-two years old.

"But I thought no exceptions for reptiles."

"Mr. Kalman had a conversation with the board," Zoe says. "See, because Mrs. Fieldstone in 203 has a Yorkie, and Mr. Garnett in 312 has a fish, and Mrs. Ettelstein in 301 has a pair of Siamese kittens, and Mr. Francis in 207 has a hamster, he argued that by discriminating against reptiles, the building was in violation of the Equal Protection Clause of the Constitution, and if they wouldn't let Benny move in, he'd sue them for emotional damages, plus legal fees of — how much do you charge an hour, Avi?"

"Four-hundred fifty dollars. Three fifty for family and friends."

"Anyway, the board backed down, so Benny's here. We picked him up yesterday from Ed's."

She leans in close, big eye to big eye. "I always prayed that someday we'd be together again."

"Good thing nobody else bought him," Alistair says.

Me, Alistair, Catalina, and Jaesang exchange looks.

"But don't tell my nana," Zoe says. "She's terrified of reptiles."

"How are you going to keep him from her?"

Mr. Kalman and Zoe smile at each other. "He's a

chameleon—they blend in. And she's half blind," they say. "She'll never know."

We gather around the terrarium and help Zoe place rocks and gravel and real plants for Benny to climb on. We unroll a wire screen, screw it to the posts, then place the lid on. We hang a heat lamp and a thermometer and a water dripper because, Zoe explains, chameleons won't drink from a bowl.

Then we watch as she sets Benny down in his new home, and I can't help thinking that if everyone takes care of Planet Earth the way Zoe is taking care of Benny, then maybe, just maybe, we'll all survive.

APPENDIX

AMENDMENTS TO THE U.S. CONSTITUTION

Excerpted & Explained by the Global Warning Kids

The first ten, also known as the Bill of Rights, were passed by Congress on September 25, 1789, and ratified by three-fourths of the states by December 15, 1791.

AMENDMENT I

Congress shall make no law respecting an establishment of religion, or prohibiting the free exercise thereof; or abridging the freedom of speech, or of the press; or the right of the people peaceably to assemble, and to petition the government for a redress of grievances.

Where do you like to pray? Temple? Mosque? Church? No place at all? In America your religion is nobody's business but yours.

Plus you get to say, write, sing, or shout whatever you want. (Just not "Fire!" when there isn't one.) You also get to group up to protest the government. Peacefully. —Alistair

AMENDMENT II

A well-regulated militia, being necessary to the security of a free state, the right of the people to keep and bear arms, shall not be infringed.

This means that citizens, who might be called on to defend the country, have the right to own guns. —Jaesang

AMENDMENT III

No soldier shall, in time of peace, be quartered in any house, without the consent of the owner, nor in time of war, but in a manner to be prescribed by law.

If we're not at war and the government wants to turn your house into a military base, or use it as an Airbnb for soldiers on leave, they can't unless you give permission. But if there's a war, they *can* take over your house. —Catalina

AMENDMENT IV

The right of the people to be secure in their persons, houses, papers, and effects, against unreasonable searches and seizures, shall not be violated, and no warrants shall issue, but upon probable cause, supported by oath or affirmation, and particularly describing the place to be searched, and the persons or things to be seized.

This says that your house—which includes your car, your backpack, your pockets, and your body parts—can't be searched without "probable cause" that you've got something illegal there. Probable cause isn't just a hunch; it's got the word *probable* in it. So, like, a 75 percent chance to be true. They've got to be so sure that they're willing to swear in front of a judge and get a warrant, or permission slip, to do the search. And they can't just search for anything; they have to name the thing they expect to find. —Sam

AMENDMENT V

No person shall be held to answer for a capital, or otherwise infamous crime, unless on a presentment of indictment of a grand jury, except in cases arising in the land or naval forces, or in the militia, when in

> *actual service in time of war or public danger; nor shall any person*
> *be subject for the same offense to be twice put in jeopardy of life or*
> *limb; nor shall be compelled in any criminal case to be a witness*
> *against himself, nor be deprived of life, liberty, or property, without*
> *due process of law; nor shall private property be taken for public use*
> *without just compensation.*

When someone says "I'm taking the Fifth," it means they have the right to remain silent when accused of a crime. The Fifth also protects you from being tried twice for the same crime. So if you're found innocent, even if new evidence comes out the next day, you can't be put back on trial for that same crime. It also protects soldiers from being tried for killing other soldiers in a time of war. One more thing about the Fifth: if the government wants to take part of your land for —I don't know, a border wall or something—they can't do it unless they pay you a fair price. —Zoe

AMENDMENT VI

> *. . . the accused shall enjoy the right to a speedy and public trial, by an*
> *impartial jury of the state and district wherein the crime shall have*
> *been committed . . . and to be informed of the nature and cause of the*
> *accusation; to be confronted with the witnesses against him; to have*

If you get arrested, you'd better understand the Sixth Amendment. It says you can't be left in jail for years while you wait for a trial. "Speedy" means soon, and if they can't try you soon, they have to let you go on bail or on a promise to show up for trial ("on his own recognizance"). The Sixth Amendment also promises that you won't be tried for a crime you don't understand and that the witnesses against you can't be anonymous; and if you have witnesses that can help you, you can force them to testify. Also, if you can't pay for a defense lawyer, the state will get you one for free. —Catalina

AMENDMENT VII

We have two kinds of courts in America: criminal and civil. You go to criminal court when you break the law; you go to civil court when you're in a fight with someone, usually over money. The Founders didn't trust judges so much, so the Seventh Amendment guarantees a trial by jury when you're fighting over more than twenty dollars.

Problem is, we don't have enough jurors to try civil disputes "in excess of twenty dollars." And civil lawsuits have gotten so expensive that most parties just settle without going to trial. The Seventh Amendment isn't as relevant as it once was. —Jaesang

AMENDMENT VIII

Excessive bail shall not be required, nor excessive fines imposed, nor cruel and unusual punishment inflicted.

The problem with excessive bail and excessive fines is that the poor wouldn't be able to afford them. Some people say the Eighth Amendment makes parking fines unconstitutional because cities charge interest for late payment. Over time, a $30 ticket can turn into a $300 bill, and if you can't pay, you go to jail. If you do go to jail, the court can't charge "excessive bail" for you to get out while waiting for your trial.

Everyone has heard of "cruel and unusual punishment." What exactly makes a punishment cruel and unusual? Is the death penalty cruel and unusual? How about forced labor for prisoners? People argue over this one a lot. —Catalina.

AMENDMENT IX

The enumeration in the Constitution, of certain rights, shall not be construed to deny or disparage others retained by the people.

Just because a right isn't protected in the Constitution doesn't mean it's not a right. The Constitution doesn't talk about the right to travel, for instance, or the right to have dogs. It doesn't say you have the right to keep private stuff private or make your own decisions about health care. So the Ninth Amendment reminds us that not every right has to be spelled out in order to be safe. —Zoe

AMENDMENT X

The powers not delegated to the United States by the Constitution, nor prohibited by it to the states, are reserved to the states respectively, or to the people.

Like the Ninth, the Tenth makes it clear that we don't want the federal government to have more power than the people give it. The only powers the federal government can have are the ones the Constitution says it can have, such as the power to raise taxes, have an army, declare war, make treaties, regulate interstate commerce, print money, establish post offices, monitor air traffic, and build and maintain roads. Everything else is up to the states. —Sam

AMENDMENT XI
Passed by Congress March 4, 1794. Ratified February 7, 1795.

> *The judicial power of the United States shall not be construed to extend to any suit in law or equity . . . against one of the United States by citizens of another state, or by citizens or subjects of any foreign state.*

Federal courts won't butt into a lawsuit against a state unless it's brought by a resident of that state. This is because our Founders didn't trust a federal government with too much power. But later Supreme Court cases have said that when it comes to civil rights, the federal courts can tell the states what to do. —Catalina

AMENDMENT XII
Passed by Congress December 9, 1803. Ratified June 15, 1804.

The electors shall meet in their respective states, and vote by ballot for president and vice president . . .

The Twelfth Amendment changes the way the Electoral College picks the president and the vice president. It used to be that the top two candidates became president and vice. But that meant you could end up with a president from one party and vice president from another, and they'd spend four years fighting with each other instead of governing together. The Twelfth Amendment fixed that by allowing parties to nominate a team. —Alistair

AMENDMENT XIII
Passed by Congress January 31, 1865. Ratified December 6, 1865.

Neither slavery nor involuntary servitude, except as punishment for crime whereof the party shall have been duly convicted, shall exist within the United States, or any place subject to their jurisdiction.

Slavery is horrible. Humanity's worst idea. The Thirteenth
Amendment outlawed it forever. —Zoe

AMENDMENT XIV

Passed by Congress June 13, 1866. Ratified July 9, 1868.

> *... nor shall any state deprive any person of life, liberty, or property*
> *without due process of law; nor deny to any person within its*
> *jurisdiction the equal protection of the laws.*

The Fourteenth Amendment rocks. It's the reason the principal
can't suspend a student without first giving them a hearing. It's the
reason you can't send white kids to nice public schools and kids of
color to crappy ones; or when you're handing out a vaccine against
COVID, you can't give it to rich people first and poor people last. It's
also why immigrants who become citizens of the United States have
the same rights as citizens who were born here. (Except they can't
become president.) —Sam

AMENDMENT XV
Passed by Congress February 26, 1869. Ratified February 3, 1870.

> *The right of citizens of the United States to vote shall not be denied or abridged by the United States or by any state on account of race, color, or previous condition of servitude.*

This amendment guaranteed Black men who had been enslaved the right to vote. But Southern states found a way around it by charging a poll tax or making people take a literacy test in order to vote. It wasn't until 1965, with the Voting Rights Act, that most Black citizens in the South could register to vote. —Jaesang

AMENDMENT XVI
Passed by Congress July 2, 1909. Ratified February 3, 1913.

> *The Congress shall have power to lay and collect taxes on incomes, from whatever source derived, without apportionment among the several states, and without regard to any census or enumeration.*

You can't run a federal government for free. You can't raise an army, build roads and bridges, manage federal lands, and enforce laws unless you get money from somewhere. Before 1913, the federal government had to share its tax revenues with the states. The Sixteenth Amendment gives it a new source of revenue—income tax—that it can keep for itself. —Catalina

AMENDMENT XVII
Passed by Congress May 13, 1912. Ratified April 8, 1913.

> *The Senate of the United States shall be composed of two senators from each state, elected by the people thereof, for six years; and each senator shall have one vote.*

Before 1913, U.S. senators were elected by the state legislators, and representatives to the House were elected by the people. But the Senate has a lot of power. It votes on the president's picks for the Supreme Court, approves of foreign treaties, and holds impeachment trials for presidents who break the law. The Constitution starts with "We the People." The Seventeenth Amendment says we the people get to pick our senators. —Zoe

AMENDMENT XVIII
Passed by Congress December 18, 1917. Ratified January 16, 1919.

After one year of the ratification of this article, the manufacture, sale, or transportation of intoxicating liquors within, the importation thereof into, or the exportation thereof from the United States . . . for beverage purposes is hereby prohibited.

The Eighteenth Amendment is the United States drunk on power. Both houses of Congress and at least thirty-eight states thought it would be a good idea to make booze illegal. What was up with those guys? Had they never tasted chicken marsala? Or penne à la vodka? Good thing that fourteen years later, they came to their senses. —Alistair

AMENDMENT XIX
Passed by Congress June 4, 1919. Ratified August 18, 1920.

The right of citizens of the United States to vote shall not be denied or abridged by the United States or by any state on account of sex.

Here's how you know the Founders of our country were men: they totally ignored women! It wasn't until 1920, with the Nineteenth Amendment, that women were officially given the right to vote. —Catalina

AMENDMENT XX

Passed by Congress March 2, 1932. Ratified January 23, 1933.

The terms of President and Vice President shall end at noon on the 20th day of January, and the terms of Senators and Representatives at noon on the 3rd day of January . . .

The Twentieth is sometimes called the Lame Duck Amendment because it shortens the time after the November election before the losers leave office and the winners take over. It's also called the "succession" amendment because it says that if the president dies in office, the vice president becomes president. —Zoe

AMENDMENT XXI

Passed by Congress February 20, 1933. Ratified December 5, 1933.

> *The eighteenth article of amendment to the Constitution of the United States is hereby repealed.*

Hurrah, we can drink again! Skål! — Betty and Mr. Kalman

AMENDMENT XXII

Passed by Congress March 21, 1947. Ratified February 27, 1951.

> *No person shall be elected to the office of President more than twice.*

George Washington really was an honest guy. Our first president could have run for a third term—and been elected for sure—but he said two terms of four years was enough for any president. It goes back to our country's suspicion of too much power in one person's hands. And for almost 150 years, presidents served only two terms at most.

But there was nothing in the Constitution that said they couldn't run for more. During the Great Depression of the 1930s, the country didn't want to change presidents, so the people elected Franklin Delano

Roosevelt four times. He was president from 1933 until he died in office in 1945.

The Republicans in Congress thought more than two terms of a Democrat was too many. So they introduced the Twenty-Second Amendment in 1947, and enough states—thirty-six was all it took because Alaska and Hawaii weren't states yet—agreed. —Jaesang

AMENDMENT XXIII
Passed by Congress June 16, 1960. Ratified March 29, 1961.

> *The District constituting the seat of Government of the United States shall appoint . . . a number of electors of President and Vice President equal to the whole number of Senators and Representatives in Congress to which the District would be entitled if it were a state.*

Basically, the Twenty-Third Amendment gives people who live in the District of Columbia the same rights to vote for president and vice president as if they lived in one of the fifty states. But it doesn't give them the right to representation in Congress. In 1978, Congress passed the District of Columbia Voting Rights Amendment, which would have given the District seats in Congress and the Senate.

258
★

But only sixteen states ratified it before the amendment expired.
—Catalina

AMENDMENT XXIV
Passed by Congress August 27, 1962. Ratified January 23, 1964.

> *The right of the citizens to vote . . . shall not be denied or abridged by the United States or any state by reason of failure to pay any poll tax or other tax.*

The Twenty-Fourth Amendment answers the Fifteenth Amendment's call for backup. It officially gets rid of the poll tax that some states charged a citizen to vote. I don't see why the government doesn't make it *easier* to vote. Like, instead of Presidents' Day being a national holiday, why isn't Election Day? —Jaesang

AMENDMENT XXV
Passed by Congress July 6, 1965. Ratified February 10, 1967.

> *Section 1. In case of the removal of the President from office or of his death or resignation, the Vice President shall become President.*

Section 2. Whenever there is a vacancy in the office of the Vice President, the President shall nominate a Vice President who shall take the office upon confirmation by a majority vote of both houses of Congress.

Section 3. Whenever the President transmits to the President pro tempore of the Senate and the Speaker of the House of Representatives his written declaration that he is unable to discharge the powers and duties of his office, and until he transmits to them a written declaration to the contrary, such powers and duties shall be discharged by the Vice President as Acting President.

Section 4. Whenever the Vice President and a majority of either the principal officers of the executive departments or of such other body of Congress may by law provide, transmit to the President pro tempore of the Senate and the Speaker of the House of Representatives their written declaration that the President is unable to discharge the powers and duties of his office, the Vice President shall immediately assume the powers and duties of the office as Acting President.

Since 1789, eight presidents have died in office—four were shot and four just died. The Constitution is clear: when a president dies, the vice president takes over. But what if the president has to have surgery, or gets really sick, and can't be president for a short time? Or what if a president goes out of his mind? You don't want a mentally disturbed person with their finger on the nuclear weapons button, do you? The Twenty-Fifth Amendment protects against these situations by making it clear as to when, and how, a president can be removed from office and when, and how, a vice president gets replaced.

It's only been used twice—both times by Richard Nixon. The first was in 1973, when his vice president, Spiro Agnew, resigned. The second was in 1974, when Nixon himself resigned. —Catalina

AMENDMENT XXVI

Passed by Congress March 23, 1971. Ratified July 1, 1971.

The right of citizens of the United States, who are eighteen years of age or older, to vote shall not be denied or abridged by the United States or any state on account of age.

This is the Vietnam era amendment that said if you're old enough to be drafted, you're old enough to vote. —Zoe

AMENDMENT XXVII

Passed by Congress September 25, 1789. Ratified May 7, 1992.

> *No law, varying the compensation for the services of the Senators and Representatives, shall take effect, until an election of representatives shall have intervened.*

I love this amendment. It shows you can be a C student and change the world. When the Founders grouped up in 1789 to plan the Constitution, Ben Franklin worried that we'd get "bold and violent personalities" who would run for office for "selfish pursuits." The flip side is, if you don't pay people in Congress for their work, only the wealthy could serve, and that wouldn't be fair.

James Madison proposed the "compensation amendment," which basically says you can't give yourself a raise. But it got only six states to ratify.

Two hundred and three years later, a college student realized that the compensation amendment didn't have an expiration date, so he got it reintroduced. And guess what. It passed! At the time, Congress's approval rating was so low, it passed easily. —Alistair

AMENDMENT XXVIII

Passed by Congress April 5, 2022. Ratified September 5, 2022.

> *A stable climate being necessary for the survival of life on Earth, the right of the people to inhabit a planet free from pollution and unnatural warming shall not be infringed.*

The Twenty-Eighth Amendment shows that even if you don't have the right to vote, you have the power to make change. It protects the planet—and the people who live on it—from a future of pollution, global warming, and mass extinction. It came from a group of kids who thought grownups weren't doing enough to stop climate change. We didn't just get mad. We took action. —Sam

GRATITUDE

How lucky to have had not one, but two editors of a book. Thank you, Margaret Raymo, for seeing the planet-in-peril as the next worthy cause for a ragtag team of kid activists to take on. And thank you, Bethany Vinhateiro, for making the transition from first editor to second so seamless and productive with your many wise contributions to this final draft.

Gratitude, as always, to Kevin O'Connor for his swift and insightful reading and steadfast support along the way.

Gratitude to Maxine Bartow for her keen eye in copyediting the manuscript; to Erika West and Lisa Lester Kelly, who saved me from my own (frequent) lapses in logic, especially when counting votes; and to my daughter Sophie, who knows the states better than I do.

Also to David Hastings and Natalie Sousa for their expertise in designing the book.

The characters in *Global Warning* are older versions of the ones in *Class Action*, but they're all dressed up in a new jacket. Thank you, Christina Chung, for a cover as beautiful to hold as it is hard to put down.

I'm also grateful to my sixth-grade students in whose company—masked or unmasked—I always find the right blend of outrage at injustice and fearlessness in wanting to fight it. It's their spirit, as much as my own, that drives the characters of this book.

To my mother-in-law, Betty Lou Ferber, whose mantra to the next generation—*MARCH!*—found its way into these pages.

To my late father, Marty Frank, for choosing a lush canyon for my childhood and for sharing his love of the Sierras with me.

To my mother, Merona Frank, for our ritual of planting bulbs in fall and beholding flowers in spring. You taught me to love—and spell—ranunculus.

To my family, including (especially?) the newest four-legged addition, Freddie Frank, for allowing me just enough space and silence to work.

Finally, to you, Reader, for your gift of attention and time.